The Determined Agent

PHILIP C. SOSSOU

authorHOUSE®

AuthorHouse™
1663 Liberty Drive
Bloomington, IN 47403
www.authorhouse.com
Phone: 833-262-8899

Published by AuthorHouse 12/11/2024

ISBN: 979-8-8230-3894-2 (sc)
ISBN: 979-8-8230-3895-9 (e)

Library of Congress Control Number: 2024925466

Print information available on the last page.

Contents

Chapter 1

Laurence Jackson and his family

Laurence Jackson came home after a long day of work. He passed his wife on the porch chatting with Gena, a neighbor's wife. He just said hello and went in. His two kids were in the backyard playing their favorite video games. His wife followed him into the house. Laurence didn't say a word.

"How was your day?" asked Bernice.

"Ok, as usual," Laurence replied. "Where are the kids?" he asked his wife. Bernice pointed to the backyard. He laid his work bag on the dining room table and went to the bedroom to remove his nice working clothes. The two kids, Joshua and Grace, ran into the house to see their dad after Bernice beckoned them. Joshua, puzzling, asked, "where is daddy?" "In the bedroom," answered Bernice, and the two kids ran into the bedroom. Laurence picked up Grace and laid his right hand on Joshua's head, walking with him into the living room where their mother sat on the old couch.

Joshua was his first son. He was six years old. He was 3 feet 10 high and was slim like his grandpa. Everybody in the family always teased him that he looked just like grandpa, Robert. He was a brilliant boy; what all his schoolteachers said the last time Laurence visited the school. Joshua had blue jeans shot on with a white t-shirt tucked into the jeans. Blue was his favorite color. He wanted his bookbag, bed hit, and shoes to be blue.

On the other hand, his younger sister Grace cared less about color now. She was four and loved reading books, especially those with pictures of princesses or Barbie. She also liked to draw. She always said she wanted to become a dentist because her dentist used to give her candies when she was little. The lady dentist loved Grace so much because she was cute and cheerful. After every visit to the dentist, Grace would draw a little dentistry with her name as a dentist. Sometimes, she would draw a picture of a lady holding some ergonomic instruments. Often, Grace would get very excited when the bedtime story had something to do with a kid at the dentist's office. She loved her dad and was much attached to him more than her brother.

The little girl cried a lot when she knew they were leaving Jonesboro for College Park. Laurence found a job as an insurance agent in Union City, a fifteen-minute drive from College Park. He had sometimes now terrible luck with his employment. His previous employer had to file bankruptcy and close the battery company, where Laurence was a line leader. Before the battery company was shut down, he saw his hours cut down to 20 hours a week. Putting food on the table was a daily struggle. Despite all the difficulty the Jackson family was going through, Laurence put himself to an insurance school, hoping to get a better job with good pay. Luckily, after certifying in Property and Casualty and Life insurance, he got a job as an insurance agent, hoping to make more money. He worked for the Greener Insurance Agency of Union City for over three years but still struggled to make ends meet. He worked hard, but all the needs in the house could not be met. The babysitter's money was taking a big chunk out of his paycheck. Laurence got rid of all unnecessary expenses, but still, life was tough for the Jacksons. They could not afford new furniture. The living room sofa was so old that the fabric lost its original color after being used for many years. The central table in the living room lost one of its legs, replaced with a plastic stick. The door handles of the old entertainment center were missing causing the little doors to open with slight movements in the living room. The old T.V. in the entertainment center could give only snowed images because Jackson could not afford the cable bill. As a result, their cable got disconnected several times. Laurence met a neighborhood hustler who knew how to work the cable system. The hustler collected $40 after a long argument over the money and assuring Laurence that his job had a long-term guarantee. Unfortunately, the cable company found out and cut the connection after two months. Then, he stopped trying. The VCR on top of the T.V. set operated manually since the kids misplaced the remote control. The dining table got fixed several times and held strong for now.

The digits on the microwave couldn't be seen anymore. They all got a hole from fingers pressing them for many years. The kids broke the toast machine on the kitchen counter, and no one was trying to get it fixed. The two children complained every morning at breakfast, but Bernice always insisted that the microwave was as good as the toaster. The top cover of the blinder still needed to be replaced. It fell accidentally on the floor and was broken. Bernice threw the broken pieces in the trash and promised to go to the thrift store on Mount Zion Road and get a used one. She went many times. Each time she purchased a blinder top cover in the thrifty store, the cover couldn't fit the base in her house, and she had to return it to the store. These were some kitchen appliances they brought from Jonesboro two years ago when they moved to College Park.

Lawrence hated seeing his wife talking to Gena, a neighbor's wife. He believed that Gena had a negative influence on her. Lately, Bernice was asking for money to buy stuff in the mall, where she accompanied Gena whenever their husbands were at work. Gena spent a lot of money on clothes and jewelry. She had a habit of mishandling money and loved designer shoes. She controlled her husband, James, and monitored his whereabouts all day.

Mr. James Colbert was a very respectful man in the community. He was the assistant manager at the chemical plant in Morrow, a little town next to Jonesboro. James was a well-educated man. He held a master's degree in chemistry from Georgia State University, one of the most outstanding institutions in the state. Mr. Colbert was making a considerable amount of money with the chemical company. His house was one of the finest furnished in the house sub-division across the street from Lawrence's apartment complex.

Everything in that house was off the latest model. At the house's entrance were two waiting rooms with a large doorway between them. A nice blue-sky carpet covered the access to the large living room. The waiting room on the right had a lovely sliding glass door with a biblical scene of the last super printed on it. It had some beautiful leather furniture and a big shelf full of books, from literature to sciences. Mr. James used the first waiting room for business partners. The second waiting room on the left was for visitors who didn't need to go into the living room. This waiting room had no door and was furnished with beautiful antique furniture. Then came a large living room after the two waiting rooms. The living room had no entertainment center but a thin smart T.V. on the wall, a brand-new leather sofa, and a couch. A bar counter was about 4 feet high and 12 feet long, surrounded by lovely leather chairs between the living room and the kitchen. Mr. James Colbert and his distinguished guests occasionally sat around the counter to eat and drink. On the other side of the kitchen was the dining room where Mr. Colbert, Gena, and their three children ate their daily meals. The kitchen had a lovely wooden floor that marked the end of the living and dining rooms. The appliances in the kitchen were all new and in good conditions. The kitchen appliances and the silverwares were clean and well-organized in the mahogany cabinets along the kitchen wall. The silverwares were neatly superposed over one another. By the side of the left waiting room mounted a wooden stairway that led to the three bedrooms upstairs. The kids' rooms were on the left, with a full bathroom in between, and the master room was on the right, facing the kids' rooms. The hallway on the top was covered with a thick green carpet that made it almost impossible to hear someone walking on the top floor. The two boys shared a bedroom, while the older girl had a room to herself. The two bedrooms were well-furnished with nice desks and computers. There was a study room at the right end of the master room that Mr. James Colbert used for his business. Below, next to the kitchen, was a white door leading to a two-car garage where the Colbert family parked their cars. There parked the two electric vehicles Mr. James Colbert owned. The new Tesla Model X model belonged to Gena and the Tesla Truck Mr. Colbert drove daily to work. A Tesla charger center was connected to the Tesla Powerwall in the garage, which Mr. James Colbert utilized to charge his two electric vehicles. Under the staircase was a WiFi room where the T.V.s and the computers in the house were connected wirelessly.

On the other hand, the Jackson family owned only an old Ford Taurus that Mr. Lawrence drove to work daily. Lawrence would drop the kids off at the babysitter's house and then drop his wife Bernice to work in the morning. Bernice would ride with a lady coworker in the afternoon and get the kids from the babysitter. Lawrence would come back home around 6:30 p.m. He worked in a large insurance agency. It was an insurance agency of two female agents working for Mr. Arnold Brown, who owned the Greener Insurance Agency. Lawrence and his colleagues worked with clients daily, writing auto and life insurance policies. Lawrence worked hard and mastered all aspects of the business. He was friendly and pleasant to all customers he got in contact with. His work was always well organized and filed in proper order. He had a delightful voice on the phone. He always explained coverage to customers so they might understand the contract they were getting into. Lawrence spent most of his day giving insurance quotes over the phone and writing insurance policies whenever customers entered the agency.

A slight mistake with an auto policy could cause much damage, and Lawrence knew that very well. An incident occurred three months after being hired as Insurance Agent at Mr. Arnold Brown's agency. Lawrence got a gentleman in the office purchasing auto insurance on a 2010 Ford F150. While writing the policy, Lawrence mistakenly keyed a wrong Vehicle Identification Number in the system. The gentleman, Randy Miller, got pulled over by a Riverdale Police Officer three weeks later. The Officer checked the VIN of the 2010 Ford F150 in the Department of Motor Vehicles system and couldn't find it. The dialogue between Randy and the Officer became an altercation because of the resentment in Randy's voice towards the Officer. The police Officer was merciless, impounded the pickup truck, and sent the gentleman home in a taxi. Randy nourished a fearless resentment toward the Riverdale police forces over a fight at a party in Riverdale. All the participants of the party, including Randy, were jailed. The event happened in the days when Riverdale police forces were trying to bring down the high crime rate in the city. A God-fearing woman, Dr. Pamela Wilson, became the mayor of Riverdale, tackled the bull by the horns, and brought down the crime rate significantly. Many businesses were trying to leave Riverdale, and the hospitals were overwhelmed with patients with gunshot wounds. After two days of investigation, the police Officer concluded there was a mistake with the Vehicle Identification Number and returned the pickup truck. Randy's parents were furious and took the young man to the insurance agency. The tow company charged $270 to let the pickup truck out of impound. Mr. Arnold Brown was in the back office when Randy and his parents showed up. Randy's mother was screaming and yelling at Lawrence for his unprofessional job. Lawrence tried everything to calm her down, but she wouldn't keep it down until Mr. Brown intervened to bring the situation under control. Lawrence's coworkers watched as if they didn't belong to the agency.

Mr. Brown paid the $270 to get the pickup truck out of the impound and deducted $50 from Lawrence's paycheck every payday until the amount was paid off. Those days were very hard for Lawrence at home and work. At work, Mr. Brown would always bring Randy's incident to his attention whenever he finished writing a new insurance policy to have him double-check all the paperwork. He had difficulty making ends meet at home; putting food on the table for his two children was challenging. Lawrence loaned money from the right and left to continue bringing food home and putting gas in his car. He even loaned some money from his next-door neighbors in the apartment complex. But he was pleased he paid everybody what he owed. For Lawrence, being free was to owe no one a dime; this was his slogan.

Chapter 2

Self Dependency

Mr. Brown was a very stingy man. He wanted all the agency money to himself. Lawrence had been begging for a raise for the last 6 months. Mr. Arnold Brown always said he would consider that next month. Then, when the next month would come around, he would say he would assume that the following month. Lawrence got tired of asking Mr. Brown to raise his salary. That was when he started thinking of getting his own insurance agency. Lawrence read many books and watched many Youtube videos on creating an insurance agency. Then, he realized he could run a successful agency and become financially independent. So, he became happy about himself. A spark would light in Lawrence's soul at the thought of being financially secure. It was something he had never experienced in his entire life and wished one day to obtain. Every night in bed, he would think of things he wanted to accomplish before he could sleep. So, he would think of a brand-new house for his two children and wife and a new car in the garage. Sometimes, Lawrence would sing a cheerful chorus with a joyful melody in his dream. His wife, Bernice, wondered what had gotten in her husband. Before leaving for work, he would sing sweet carols of bright future tunes in the shower. One night, Lawrence called his wife to the dining table after his children went to bed.

"I have figured out," Lawrence started, "what I should be doing."

"What's it?" answered Bernice, his wife.

"We have been suffering to raise our two children and have a decent home for a long time," continued Lawrence.

"You are doing the best you can for us," added Bernice.

"Now, I need to open my own insurance agency," he added. There was a moment of silence. Lawrence looked at his wife to read the thoughts going through her mind. She became emotional in her trembling voice but couldn't let out any drop of tears. Then, with a body gesture, she took control of herself.

"But it requires start-up capital!" Bernice instinctively injected.

"I spoke with a long-time friend of mine at Bank of America who promised to help me secure a loan from the Bank."

"Yeah?........ "Bernice asked.

"I have already applied for consideration," Lawrence continued.

Then, there was a long silence while Bernice looked deep at the dinner table. Many images were flooding her mind, and some questions did surface. The dominant concern was the agency's inability to generate enough money to pay back the loan. But she suppressed those negative thoughts and said to herself, "please, focus on the bright sight." Both stood up at the same time and embraced one another for about three minutes without saying anything, and then walked together slowly to the bedroom.

The next day, Lawrence organized a consultation with the Georgia Department of Insurance's commissioner to review the agency licensing procedure. The Georgia Department of Insurance was located at the heart of Downtown Atlanta. It was a tall brown building with the Commissioner's office on the 12th floor. The Commissioner was busy that morning, and he couldn't receive Lawrence. But his secretary had to rearrange the situation for Lawrence to meet with the Deputy of the Commissioner. The meeting turned out to be very successful, according to Lawrence. The Deputy was very nice, explained all the licensing details, and gave Lawrence different recommendations as far as the A++ reinsures were concerned. After the meeting, Lawrence went to work, where many customers waited in the lobby. He came in with a bright smile on his face. He thought about how happy he would be to see his own insurance agency full of customers every morning. He was still thinking about how fairly he would treat his employees when Mr. Brown called him from the back office to tell him that everyone in the lobby was waiting for him. His coworkers were making the gesture of saying, "help us now, partner." In an hour, they reduced the number of customers to two. Then he stood to use the restroom in the back of the office. A thought hit him loud and clear as he pushed his chair backward: "why couldn't you use that energy for your own good?". Lawrence turned to look at his coworkers to see if they had heard the voice that went through him. But no one paid him attention; all were still busy helping the customers. He passed Mr. Brown's office before getting to the bathroom. He saw Mr. Brown counting his money and organizing a stack of money in a safe in his office. Lawrence came back from the restroom to take care of the last customer. Lawrence just sat quietly by his desk smiling inside. He was contemplating how much money he would make and how he would take good care of his family. His wife always wanted a nice wedding ring which she couldn't have because they couldn't afford one. When money started coming in, he would have a ceremony to renew his vow to his wife with a diamond ring. After all the customers had left, Lawrence expected many questions from his colleagues about why he was so late this morning or where he went, but no one asked about his tardiness. Lawrence went to his boss before leaving for the day to ask for a day-off in the following week. After a heated argument, Mr. Brown finally agreed to grant him the coming Wednesday because Wednesdays were the slowest days of the week regarding customer volume. The following Wednesday, Lawrence went to see a bank official of Bank of America with his wife to sign paperwork for his business loan. The loan conditions were tight, and Lawrence couldn't qualify for the $50,000 business credit line. The Bank needed a guarantee or collateral before it could approve the loan. The loan officer Jimmy sat down with the couple to review all the alternatives and how Lawrence's loan application could be approved. After the meeting with Jimmy, the couple decided to bring in Bernice's father to co-sign the loan. In the Bank's parking lot, Bernice called her father to warn him that they were coming to see him for a serious matter the following Sunday after church. Bernice knew his father well that Sundays were the best days anyone could easily get money from her dad. Bernice's father and mother, Andrew and Liz Dove, lived in

Cobb County in a three-bedroom house they managed to pay off before retirement. Andrew and Liz retired from the Cobb County Public School System, where Andrew taught Geometry in high school, and Liz taught English Arts at East Cobb Middle School. Before the school system, Andrew worked for many years for the Cobb County Post Office. While working in the post office sorting mails, Andrew put himself to school. He loved mathematics when he was in high school. He enrolled in the math department at Kennesaw State University, where he graduated in Applied Mathematics. After graduating, he retired from the post office and became a Math teacher at Campbell High School. Besides their social security money and the school system pension, Andrew accumulated a lot of money with the Federal Government during his post office years. After resigning from the post office job, he didn't touch his pension until he turned 65. He let the money accrue until his full retirement year. Andrew and Liz spent their retirement days turning their backyard into a colorful garden. They spent a lot of time and money planting flowers and would get very enthusiastic whenever one of their three children came home to visit. Before they went to church on the Sunday of the visit, Liz woke up early to cook for the Jackson family. Liz was so happy to see again the two children, Joshua and Grace. Andrew wasn't so ruffled about the visit because he knew Bernice would always visit whenever she had a money problem. Cooking and baking for the Jackson family made Liz and Andrew late to church, which generated verbal arguments in the car. Andrew didn't like attending church late, but Liz didn't consider that an offense to the Lord. For her, the Lord knew the reason they were late.

By 3:00 p.m. Lawrence, his wife, and the two children arrived in their old Ford Taurus at the Dove residence. The whole house smelled delicious food. After the hugging and the greetings, Liz grabbed Bernice's right hand, pulling her to the kitchen: "I need your help in the kitchen before we eat." There were different types of dishes wrapped up in aluminum foil in the kitchen. Liz and her daughter moved the plates to the dining room while Lawrence and Andrew chatted.

"You're still working for the insurance company?" asked Andrew.

"Yes, I'm still working there," answered Lawrence.

"How is life treating you there?" continued Andrew.

"Not bad, I'm hanging there," affirmed Lawrence.

"Let us know if there is anything we can do to help," Andrew widened the floor of the conversation.

"We know we can count on you, that's ....." Lawrence didn't finish his sentence before Liz and Bernice started calling them to the dining room. The dining table was set up correctly. There were various dishes in the middle and plates with silverware. The Jacksons were sitting on one side of the table while the Doves were on the other side, facing one another. Liz passed the salad around and then the rest of the dishes one after the other. Then, in the middle of the eating and drinking, Bernice brought out the reason for their visit. She explained how the bank needed someone to co-sign a loan application so Lawrence could start his own insurance agency. He had been working for the Arnold Brown Agency for over five years, and it was time to get his own agency. Bernice urged her father to bring his monthly statement for his social security benefits, pension, and annuities to the Bank on Wednesday at 9:00 a.m., the next appointment. Liz agreed that was an excellent idea but wanted to know what would happen when Lawrence couldn't pay the loan back. Lawrence couldn't convince her mother-in-law, despite his explanation of how lucrative the insurance business was. Finally, Andrew agreed to bring all his financial statements to the Bank at the appointment time. Liz and Andrew wouldn't let the Jacksons go until late that night. Liz had called Bernice's other two siblings, one in California and the other in New Jersey. Lawrence spent a reasonable amount of time on the phone with his in-laws. The Jacksons went home with a lot of cooked food packed in plastic containers and put in the trunk of their old Ford Taurus. Liz didn't have anyone to eat the leftover, so she would rather give them to her daughter and the two children.

Wednesday morning, when Jimmy, the loan officer, saw how much Andrew had in the Fed retirement account, he was amazed. He just went to the Xerox machine, made a copy of all the financial paperwork Andrew brought, and created a business account with a $50,000 deposit for Lawrence. The Bank's primary concern was to monitor the use of the money to make sure that the money would be used for business purposes.

The next day, at the end of his shift, Lawrence went to Mr. Arnold Brown in his office to give him a two-week notice to vacate his position as an insurance agent. Mr. Brown was upset and troubled by the notice but didn't know what to say. Three weeks later, Lawrence went to rent an office in a commercial center on Riverdale Road next to a busy Asian grocery market in College Park and brought a copy of the rental agreement to the Bank as was stipulated in the contract. It would take another three weeks before the office would be ready for business. And his landlord offered him the first month rent-free. In the meantime, his approval letters with the insurer were in the mail. He contracted with Infinity Reinsurer Group, which helped him with the business guarantee. Lawrence couldn't believe that he was on his way to the mountain top. He vowed to himself to do everything possible to get his head above the water.

Chapter 3

The tragedy of Margret Wade

L awrence's mother, Katina Jackson, was a strong woman who dedicated her energy and strength to the wellbeing of her three children. Lawrence and his two siblings had a rough childhood. Everything was going well for Lawrence's family until the unexpected even occurred. Lawrence's father, Robert Jackson, was an aircraft maintenance technician working for the IAG company at Hartford International Airport in Atlanta. He went through aircraft maintenance technician training right after his high school graduation. He completed the training and passed the corresponding state exams with the airport administration. His company contracted with Delta Airlines, American Airlines, and Horizon Airlines. Robert quickly mastered his job and was good at it. After two years on the job, he got promoted to a leadership position. His schedule had changed, and he worked the day shift from 8:30 a.m. to 5:00 p.m. Monday through Friday. Robert loved that schedule, allowing him to spend more time with his three children, Laura, Mike, and Laurence. Robert would catch Bus 330 from Old National Highway straight to the airport in the morning. He always made it on time and had always been on time. Going home in the evening, Robert would get the same Bus 330, around 5:20 p.m., from Atlanta Airport going to Fayette County, passing through College Park. Every evening Robert rode Bus# 330 with a homeless woman named Margaret. Margaret had never wanted to sit in the bus. She preferred standing in the bus whether it was empty or full. Margret would hold on to an iron bar in the bus with her right hand and holding a large plastic bag containing her belonging with her left hand. She wouldn't say anything to anybody or answer anyone's questions. Margret always stayed quiet no matter what was going on around her. A fight broke out in the bus next to Margret one day, and the bus driver thought she would say something. Margret moved away from the fight holding firmly the iron bar and her plastic bag. The bus driver tried everything to get her to say something, but he was unsuccessful in all his attempts in the three years he had known the homeless woman. Sometimes, Margret reminded herself to ring the bell in the bus to request a stop. The bus driver knew she was supposed to get off at the corner of Old National Highway and Flat Shoals Road, where was an abused women's shelter. Margret went there every evening to eat her last meal of the day, freshen up, then take the Bus 330 back to Downtown Atlanta, where she would sleep under a bridge. She utilized the plastic bag containing her belongings as a pillow. In the morning, Margret put the plastic bag in a shopping cart that she pushed around. She walked around Downtown aimlessly. Whenever she met any other homeless person, she would socialize for a little while and then move on. People would like to know what they could talk about. The bus driver tried to crack the mystery behind Margret's mental problem, and he always thought about her. He couldn't understand what had pushed this gorgeous young woman to the street. Maybe she didn't have any Atlantean relatives who could rescue her. "So, why couldn't she hold a decent job? Maybe her mental capacity can't allow her to maintain a job position," thought Reginald, the bus driver. All homeless people went through something that made them the way they shouldn't be. They all had a story to tell.

Behind her dirty appearance, Margret was a beautiful woman of about 32 years. She was a Caucasian lady, slim and tall. Margret looked like someone with much potential. She walked majestically as a lady from a royal family. A purple sweater and tight blue jeans were what she wore every day. One day Margret stopped taking the bus. For about a week, Margret didn't board Bus 330. Reginald looked for her, waited for her, and didn't see a sign of Margret. Reginald had a feeling that something wrong had happened to Margret. He didn't know whom to ask. So, Reginald thought about calling the police to report the disappearance of Margret. He was confident that something terrible had happened to the homeless lady. But Reginald didn't have any evidence to tell the police. Margret's disappearance hunted Reginald so much that he started dreaming about her in different scenarios almost every night. Reginald dreamt of driving Bus 330 and chatting with Margret onboard. The two were having a conversation until Margret forgot her bus stop. But Reginald knew very well her stop. He stopped at the right stop and opened the rear door for Margret, who smiled at him and said "thank you, you're a real friend" for the first time.

Reginald woke up in the morning trying to figure out the meaning behind the dream. He knew not every dream meant something and hoped this one was meaningless. Reginald convinced himself not to have anything to do with that homeless woman. Indeed, he brushed it off and tackled his day as usual, forgetting everything about Margret until he went to work at 2:00 p.m. Reginald started his shift with a bus full of people servicing the line between Fayette County and Downtown Atlanta. When he reached the stop where he usually picked Margret up every evening, three Atlanta police Officers stopped the bus and ordered Reginald to come down for questioning. He was shocked and confused. Many thoughts were racing through his mind, and hot sweat ran down his cheek. Two male police Officers and a female Officer surrounded Reginald when he got off the bus. The female officer handed him a California driver's license with a beautiful Caucasian woman picture. The female Officer asked him if he could recognize the photo of the driver's license. At first, Reginald didn't recognize the face in the picture, and he said he didn't know who that was. Then, the men's Officers asked Reginald if the name on the driver's license rang a bell or meant anything to him. The name on the driver's license read: Margret Abigail Wade and the address was: 9782 South Vermont Avenue, Torrance, CA. That was when Reginald could connect the dots.

"This is the picture of Margret, the homeless woman who rides my bus every evening around 5:00 p.m. to College Park," answered Reginald.

"Do you know anything about her?" the female officer asked.

"No, she doesn't talk to anybody. If I ask her any questions, she'll not answer," added Reginald.

"She is found dead this morning under the bridge, and we're trying to find her relatives," continued the Officer.

"I have seen her talking to other homeless people at the bus stop," affirmed Reginald.

"We have spoken to all the homeless people, and they say they haven't any information about her relatives. But they see her taking the Bus 330 every evening to eat in College Park. That's why we stop you for questioning," state the Officers.

"What is the cause of her death?" asked Reginald.

"The autopsy shows no signs of trauma and affirms pneumonia. Besides, we have found money in her plastic bag with dirty clothes," stated the officers.

"How much money you're talking about, if I may ask?" asked Reginald.

"We counted $80,000. That's why we need to find the origin of the money," concluded the Officers who took off in their marked patrol car.

The next day, the Sheriff's office got involved in Margret Wade's case. It was uncommon occurrence that a homeless woman would have $80k cash in a plastic bag. The sheriff's office in Atlanta faxed Margret's driver's license to the Sheriff's office in Los Angeles to go to the address and find any deceased's relatives. When two Sheriffs knocked at the 9782 South Vermont Avenue door, an old lady came to the door.

"Hi, mam, we're the Sheriffs. How're you doing?" the two agents presented their respective badges and IDs.

"Fine," the old lady said, moving her two eyes from one Sheriff to another. There was a long silence.

"Can we come in, please?" the two Sheriffs said.

"Why?" the old lady asked. One of the Sheriffs retrieved an enlarged color copy of Margret's driver's license to show her. The shock on the lady's face made her jaw drop instantly. She couldn't say a word but opened the door for the two Sheriffs to enter. Then, as soon as the agents stepped in, the door locked behind them as if somebody was watching them. So, she called her husband, who was in the bedroom when the Sheriffs knocked at the door. Margret's parents, John and Carroll Wade, lived in a one-bedroom apartment. They had a nice living room with a glass center table with artificial fruits like apples, bananas, grapes, oranges, and more. The living room TV was sitting on a small table against the wall. A desk with a laptop computer and a printer was in the far corner of the living room. A small kitchen was on the opposite side of the living room. It was hot in the apartment. The air conditioning wasn't working or turned off. It felt moggy inside, for the windows had never been opened to get the air to circulate through the apartment. The couple lived on a fixed income and didn't waste much money on utilities. The carpet in the apartment was covered with transparent plastic from the entrance door to the bedroom. The dining room had one small table with two chairs that faced one another. Carroll had food on the stove before the Sheriffs came. There were a sofa and a loveseat in the living room. They looked new and had transparent plastic bags to keep them from dirt. They had the two Sheriffs sitting on the sofa while they sat on the loveseat. The look on the face of the couple was intense. One of the Sheriffs handed them the color copy of Margret's California driver's license.

"Do you know the lady in the photo?" asked the Sheriff holding a yellow folder.

"This is our daughter Margret" without hesitation, answered John.

"What has happened to Margret?" asked John, his eyes wide open.

"We're very sorry that she's no more. She's at the Grady Hospital, and the autopsy shows she died from pneumonia," the Sheriff answered.

At this point, Carroll was on the floor, rolling in tears. John couldn't hold the tears that were dripping down his face. With tears dripping on his chest, John still had firmly Margret's driver's license photocopy in his hand. The two Sheriffs were overwhelmed by the situation and were trying to contain themselves.

"She collects $100,000 of her husband's death benefit and leaves for Georgia, and we have never heard from her since," added John.

The two Sheriffs explained to Margret's parents that she had become homeless in Atlanta sleeping under a bridge. She got sick and didn't go to the hospital until the Atlanta police found her dead one morning. The police found $80 000 in her bag. The two Sheriffs collected a sample of John and Carroll's hair and saliva for a DNA test to establish a parental relationship with Margaret. After the DNA, the Wades would come to Atlanta to collect the money and proceed with the burial. Carroll loved her daughter dearly. She was working at McDonald's when she married Jacob Beavers. Jacob was working for a trucking company in Carson. He was a forklift operator for the ABC company. He was loading an eighteen-wheeler while the truck driver unknowingly drove off. The forklift fell one foot high from the dock to the outside ground. The forklift fell on Jacob's chest and broke all his right ribs, causing internal bleeding. He was rushed to the hospital, in a three-day coma, and passed away. The company paid for the hospital expenses, the worker compensation benefit, and the company life insurance. The company paid Margret, the beneficiary, $100,000 a day after the burial. Margret's hands were shaking when she brought home the cash money from Wachovia bank. That was the first time she had had a colossal amount of money. She promised herself to take good care of this money. She would keep the money to herself and not use it. Before leaving for Georgia, Margret gave her parents $10,000 and took a Greyhound Bus to Atlanta, Georgia, where she knew no one. She used only $10,000 for all the three years she had been living on Atlanta's streets. She kept the rest of the money in a plastic bag with some of her clothes as a pillow.

Two days later, the Sheriff's office in Atlanta called John Wade to come and collect the $80,000 found on Margret and organize the burial in Atlanta. At the news, Garfield, Margret's older brother, came from Denver-Colorado to travel with his parents to Atlanta. Garfield was the first child of the Wade family, and he opened a Pizza business in Denver. Two days after the call from the Sheriff's office in

Atlanta, the trio took a Delta aircraft 757 to the Hartsfield-Jackson International Airport. The three took a taxi from the airport to the Sheriff's headquarters in Atlanta and presented their identification cards to collect money. After that, they went to the Grady Hospital to view the body of their beloved Margret. Then they purchased a burial plot in the Forest Park National Cemetery for $15,000 for the burial. Garfield couldn't understand the passing of his younger sister. His father explained how Margaret became greedy after she collected the insurance money of $100,000. It was an amount she had never had before, and she would do anything to keep it to herself. She wanted to move to a city where no one knew her. She was debating between Florida and Georgia. Finally, she chose Georgia, where the cost of living wasn't so high. She was saying she could get a cheap apartment in downtown Atlanta and buy groceries at a low price. Her parents tried to pursue her, but the drive inside of her was so strong that no one could convince her. She went to the Torrance Greyhound Bus Station and started on the journey that led her to the Forest Park National Cemetery. Garfield and his parents cried for a long time at the cemetery. They left Georgia with the rest of Margaret's money in the amount of fifty thousand dollars.

Garfield and Margaret were Mr. and Mrs. Wade's only children. The two had a flourishing childhood. They were inseparable and did everything together. Garfield was the older one, and Margaret followed him everywhere he went. From elementary through high school, they went to the school. After Torrence High School, Garfield continued his education at El Camino College while Margaret decided to enter the workforce. College was challenging for Garfield, but he managed to pull it through. In his senior year, Garfield took a Chemistry class he intensely hated. Although he wasn't a fan of chemistry, Garfield loved a girl in the chemistry class. Garfield wanted to drop the class, but his affection for Melanie Burns kept him coming on time.

Garfield admired everything about Melanie. He never dared to engage in a conversation with her. Garfield pretended not to acknowledge the girl's presence for fear of rejection. One day, Garfield was the last student to complete his class assignment. The rest of the class finished the assignment and left. On her way to her next class, Melanie realized she left her book in the chemistry class. By the time she returned to the chemistry class, Garfield was on his way out of the class. The two students met face to face at the door of the chemistry class alone. Garfield seized the opportunity to engage Melanie in a one-on-one conversation to find out that Melanie also had a feeling for him. It turned out that the two students were pursuing an Associate Degree in Business Management. To Garfield's amazement, the two students had a lot in common as far as plans for the future were concerned. Melanie and Garfield started dating and spent many hours on the phone daily. Garfield presented his new fiancée to John and Carrol Wade, who warmly received the news. Although Margaret wasn't too receptive in the first place, but finally welcomed Melanie with open arms.

Melanie lived with her mother in Denver, Colorado, where her father owned a big house before passing away. She shared a room in a house in Gardena California, half a mile from El Camino College. Melanie always returned home to her mother every school break or every long weekend. She was the only child of her parents, and her mother loved her dearly after her father passed away from a heart surgery. Garfield and Melanie studied together and planned their future together. After their associate degree in Business Administration, Garfield moved in with Melanie and turned the basement of her father's house into a pizza factory. Mrs. Burns, Melanie's mother, purchased the first dough-making machine and the first sac of wheat flour to launch the business. Garfield would make the pizza, and Melanie would make the delivery, as she knew the city of Denver as if it were the back of her hand. The pizza business was booming, and Mrs. Burns had to take some calls and help with the delivery. The company was making a lot of money, so Garfield and Melanie had to move out of the basement and rent space in downtown Denver. They used the basement to stock merchandise and inventory. Garfield hired two employees to take his business to another level. Garfield received the call about Margaret's death in the middle of excitement of higher production of his pizza business.

Chapter 4

From the mountain top to the valley

Katina Jackson worked for a Kroger grocery store not far from her house. She worked forty hours a week for the grocery store. She worked from 7:00 a.m. to 3:00 p.m. from Monday through Friday. Katina loved working for the store because she could buy everything she needed at home at an employee's discounted price. She walked home with two or three plastic bags full of groceries daily. She also loved her schedule because she wanted to be home before her three children returned from school. She wanted to ensure that her children had their homework done before bedtime. Lawrence's mother always ensured that she had ice cream and animal crackers in the house before the school bus would drop her children at the front of the apartment complex. Laura, Mike, and Lawrence craved a snack whenever they returned from school and got rid of their book bags. The Jackson family lived in a three-bedroom apartment on Old National Highway. Laura was the oldest of the three, and Lawrence was the youngest. They all attended Banneker High School in College Park. Laura was in 11th, Mike in 10th, and Lawrence in 9th. Their father made enough money as an aircraft maintenance technician to meet his household's ever-increasing financial demands. Before Robert could get home in the evening, Katina would prepare a delicious meal for the whole family. The children expressed concerns about the school or the neighborhood at the dinner table. Sundays were a fun time to go to the amusement park. Robert and Katina were a happy couple who didn't have much and who didn't lack anything. One Saturday morning, Robert got called to work because of a workforce shortage; an employee called out last minute. He hated working on weekends because the buses ran mostly late. Bus 330 ran on a schedule of one hour on the weekend. If Robert happened to miss a bus, it would take him another hour to catch the next one. Robert was maintaining a Horizon aircraft 787 and found a crack in the left wing. He wanted to ground the aircraft, but his shift was about to end, and he didn't have enough time to file the appropriate paperwork. Robert didn't want to miss his bus either. He decided to implement a quick fix and patch the hole in the left wing with crazy glue. He clocked out and ran to the bus station, Bus 330 going to Fayette County. On the bus, Robert prayed that the Atlanta Falcon's game with the Dolphins shouldn't be over before he reached home. His two boys were watching the game before he got home. Katina cooked rice, oxtails with gravy, fried beef livers, and corn. Before Robert walked in, she set the table with all the food, and the whole house smelled good. Katina pulled the whole family around the table while watching the football game on the TV. After dinner, Robert was glued to the TV all night because the game was tough, and they went to overtime twice before the Falcons prevailed. He listened to the journalist commentators of the game until late that night. The next morning, Robert woke up and went to the TV set, hoping to hear more comments on the last night's game between the Atlanta Falcons and the Miami Dolphins. To his surprise, there was nothing about the Falcons or the Dolphins. Some news about Horizon's 787 aircraft crashed the previous night shortly after leaving the Hartsfield-Jackson International Airport. Robert flipped through all the channels; they covered the tragic loss of the 120 passengers on board the aircraft. The journalists said the pilot reported malfunctioning of the aircraft's left wing. Suddenly, a mountain of guilt poured on Robert from head to toes, and he became sick with a high fever. He lost his appetite for everything. Robert returned to bed without breakfast and covered himself with a heavy blanket. In the afternoon, Katina and the three children tried to wake him up so they could go to their regular playground. They couldn't wake him up, and they went outside by themselves. The next morning, Katina woke him up to shower and go to work. Robert was too ill to go to work, and Katina urged him to call his job and report that he was sick. He didn't call his job and rather turned his cell phone off. The following day, Robert received a message from his boss: "You need to call me, and we need to talk. I have been waiting for you since yesterday". His sickness went to his head when he played the message on his cellphone. He said to himself: "All my co-workers are aware that I'm responsible for the plane crash." In the afternoon, Robert found a liquor store at the corner of Old National Highway and Godby Road. He drank heavily at the liquor store until 3:00 a.m. before returning home. Katina confronted him to know what was happening to him. Robert became violent and aggressive and would leave home for three or five days. He would return dirty and drunk. Katina couldn't pay the rent monthly, yet a second eviction notice was taped to her door. That was when she started calling different governmental institutions for help. Finally, Katina contacted the mental health department chief officer, who found a place for Robert at the Lakeview Behavioral Health Center in Norcross, Georgia. Robert was treated at the mental health center, but his case worsened. A month later, Katina took her three children to visit their father at the mental health center. The visitation wasn't a pleasant one. Robert couldn't recognize any of his family members. He lost weight and looked at his children as strangers. He looked like a man in his early seventies. Katina and the children were weeping on their way back to find another eviction notice on their door. The next morning, Katina went to the Leasing Office to see the manager and exposed the situation she found herself in. The manager decided to move the Jacksons out of the three-bedroom apartment to a one-bedroom apartment which would be more affordable for the family. Then Katina took a bus to Upper Riverdale, where she applied for a cashier position in an Aldi grocery store. The store had been looking for a cashier for a long time and retained Katina the same day for orientation. Joggling between two jobs wasn't easy for Katina and the high school students. Katina had to be at the ALDI store by 8:00 a. m. and worked at the Kroger store from 4:30 p.m. to 9:00 p.m. to afford the rent and put food on the table for the children. Katina worked six days a week and had no time for her children except Sundays. But Sundays were her only days of rest, and she slept all day long, and no one was there to follow the academic performance of the children or respond to parent conferences with the teachers. Katina had no time to cook anymore, and the children had to cook their food. Lawrence was good at fixing Macaroni and Cheese; Mike preferred fried chicken with French fries, whereas Laure adored gravy with oxtail and cooked rice.

Katina would buy the grocery, and the children would cook the dishes and clean the house. The children spent more time playing video games and watching TV with no father figure in the house. Life in Jackson's family had changed drastically. Now, the children were wearing the same clothes to school every day. Their phone lines were discontinued; only Katina had a phone for an emergency calls. The weekly allowance for the children was taken away. The Comcast cable box and the internet were disconnected, and the electric bill was only paid whenever the Georgia Power sent in a disconnection notice. Some of the homework required an internet connection, and the students had to wait until Saturday to go to the library to use the computer.

Katina was working in the ALDI store when her phone rang one morning. She hesitated to pick up the call because she didn't know who was calling. After a while, she picked up the call.

"Hello!" Katina answered the call with a solid and deep voice.

"Is this Mrs. Katina Jackson?" the voice on the other end of the line asked.

"This is she; who're you?" replied Katina. It was a friendly female voice on the other end, which Katina couldn't recognize.

"Do you remember me now? I'm Mrs. McKey, the manager of the mental health center in Norcross.

"Oh, I do remember you now," said Katina.

"Where are you now? I want to talk to you in a secured area," continued Mrs. McKey. Katina knew something was wrong with her husband. The conditions in which she saw him the last time she and the children visited him weren't promising.

"I'm in a grocery store. Give me a minute or two to get outside," Katina added when she got outside to the back of the building.

"Hello, are you there, Mrs. McKey?".

"Yes, I'm here," said Mrs. McKey. There was a slight pause. So many thoughts were running through Katina.

"Now, tell me, what's wrong with my Husband?" instated Katina.

"It's so hard for me to tell you exactly what has happened. A nurse found him this morning unconscious in his bed. She tried CPR on him, but he wasn't responding. The nurse called his physician, who confirmed that Robert was no more". At this point, Katina's cell phone dropped out of her right hand. Her jaw dropped, and tears started running down her cheeks. Her throat got dry and tightened so hard that she couldn't utter a word. When Katina bent down to pick up the phone, she realized that Mrs. McKey was still talking. She discussed the funeral arrangements to bury Robert in the Norcross National Cemetery. Katina promised the lady on the phone that she would be there the next day to oversee all the preparations for the burial. After the phone conversation, Katina went to the ALDI store manager to break the news and took a bus home with tears in her eyes. As soon as she got home, Katina called the Kroger store management to inform them of the loss of her husband. The idea came to Katina to contact Robert's job to inquire about any life insurance policy he might have. She managed to get in touch with the AISG manager at Hartsfield-Jackson International Airport, Robert's direct boss. He informed Katina that Robert had been terminated for three days of no-call no-show. The policy required him to call the job anytime he wouldn't make it to work. He didn't reach out to his supervisor to report that he was sick and wouldn't return any calls when the job had called. The boss had called his phone many times to ask him about a negligent job he did by gluing a piece of metal on a 787 aircraft. The plane captain found the damage in the left wing and grounded it for further check-ups. The plane couldn't fly out of Hartsfield-Jackson International Airport and was still being worked on in the airfield depot of the Atlanta airport.

Katina was sitting at the dining table with dry tear traces on her face when her three children came home from school. They were all confused to see their mother home at 3:00 p.m., and her two arms crossed over her head. Laura busted into tears at the bad news, but Mike and Lawrence were in disbelief, not grasping the magnitude of the loss. Katina and Laura were mourning for the rest of the afternoon. The following day, Katina and Laura took an Uber to the mental health center where Robert had been receiving treatment for the last three months. His body couldn't be kept in the center for over three days. The view of the dead body was programmed on the following morning. The burial was in the afternoon at the Norcross National Cemetery. The state reimbursed the Lakeview Behavioral Health Center for the total cost because Jackson had no money to pay. The next day,

Robert's family was there to view the body and proceeded to the burial in Norcross National Cemetery. The ALDI store and the Kroger store sent in, respectively, a representative. The two representatives brought a significant support in an envelope, a token of appreciation during a hard time.

After the burial of Robert's body, Katina became seriously ill from standing up for an extended time every day at work, and her feet were swelling. She was in intensive care for two years at the Riverdale Memorial Hospital. Laura couldn't finish her senior year at Banneker High School and started working as a cashier at a Kroger Grocery store. She became the primary source of income for the family. She would bring groceries home every evening after work and share the responsibility among siblings. Laura was a great cook in the image of her mother. She organized the visitation of her mother every weekend at Riverdale Memorial Hospital. Laura managed to hold her family together until her mother was released from the hospital and resumed her activities. Soon after, Laura got engaged to a truck driver and moved to Los Angeles, California. She called her mother every weekend to check on her. Mike and Lawrence found it challenging to attend a class every day because life had become unbearable. So, Mike dropped out of school and started a carrier as a mechanic to contribute to the family's needs. Lawrence managed to get his high school diploma and went to Robert Thomas Insurance Institute of Atlanta after working few years with the Trojan Battery Company. He passed the State Exam of Life and Property & Casualty and got a job in the Greener Insurance Agency owned by Mr. Arnold Brown in Union City. He was brilliant in life and automobile insurance and was knowledgeable in different aspects of insurance practices.

Chapter 5

The new insurance agency

The Infinity Reinsurer Group had sent different posters to Lawrence for his new agency. He organized the agency very neatly. He made a waiting area separated from his writing desk with a glass wall. The waiting room was very nice; the customers could sit at a glass table full of magazines. The wall on the left and right had a stand for advertising brochures and flyers. The writing area consisted of a desk with two computers: one laptop and one desktop. Next to the desktop was a cash register. Under the desk was a printer with a scanner. In the back were three tall file cabinets where Lawrence had yellow folders containing the information of all his clients. There was a door from the waiting room to the writing area, which was always locked. Lawrence's office was in the back of the agency, where he kept his money in a safe. Next to his office was the restroom. Bernice Jackson was very excited about the opportunity and put herself into the advertisement aspect of the business. She went to an Office Depot to order numerous flyers, business cards, and banners. Every morning, Bernice would go to supermarkets' parking lots to put flyers on cars calling drivers to get a quote with the new insurance agency. She took her aggressive approach online too. She was on Facebook, Instagram, Twitter, and more. The phone started ringing after a while, and people came to the Lawrence-Jackson insurance agency to purchase auto insurance. Lawrence was courteous and willing to work with his customers if they had problems. Two months after the opening of the Lawrence-Jackson Insurance Agency, Lawrence couldn't take all the calls coming in, and his answering machine was full every day before he would leave the office. Instead, he planned to hire a young lady that could handle all his calls. Bernice didn't like the idea and quit her part-time job to work in her husband's agency as a Customer Service Representative. Bernice didn't like the job, not because she couldn't handle the phone calls but because of the environment. Bernice became so overprotective of her husband. This was the first time Bernice saw a bright light in her marriage. Finally, she saw potential prosperity in her way. Her love for Lawrence went up to the roof. Bernice couldn't stand that girls were coming to the office trying to hit on Lawrence and making open advances on her husband. Instead, she fought with a lady trying to seduce Lawrence. Bernice couldn't contain herself and didn't know when she grabbed the lady by the neck and threw her on the floor in the waiting room. When she came back to her senses, she apologized to the lady. After the incident, Lawrence urged his wife not to come to the agency anymore. Then, Lawrence hired a young Latina girl who handled all the calls and gave quotes to potential clients over the phone and online. Brenda Morales, the new girl, was enthusiastic and energetic like her boss. They both got along just fine. Then Lawrence started to unfold his plan. Lawrence would slide a life policy of $50,000 face amount on some of his customers' auto insurance policies and make his agency a primary and sole beneficiary. He carefully selected who should have a life rider according to the client's age, sex, and location. He assigned a unique file cabinet for all the auto policies with a life policy embedded in them. In that cabinet, Lawrence got detailed personal information about those customers. He had accurate details about his clients: people who lived with them, when they were usually home, and their work schedules. He even had the city map quested the targeted customers' addresses in color. After his agency closed at 5:00 p.m., Lawrence stayed in the back office to study the environment of his victims once or twice at night. When his wife asked why he came home late, Lawrence replied that he had much work to finish. He ordered a FN 509 Compact Tactical 9mm Pistol and ammunition online sent to the address of his agency. He kept the pistol and ammunition in the safe where the business money was held before being deposited in a bank.

Lawrence Jackson had targeted a young single mother of one named Michelle Cornett, who purchased auto insurance with Lawrence a month ago. Michelle was an ideal candidate for Lawrence's Machiavellian plan. At the time of the auto insurance contract, Lawrence slid a life insurance policy on the agreement without Michelle's consent. He made the Lawrence Jackson insurance agency the beneficiary for the face amount of $50,000. Michelle was a young and beautiful woman, an assistant manager at College Park Walmart, who lived with her son Brendon. Michelle finished high school when she had her first child at age eighteen. She never had a chance for a long-lasting relationship. She had dated several men but couldn't find one who would treat her like the queen she was meant to be. Then she stopped looking for a dream guy and focused all her attention and care on her son. Brendon was the sun in her life, and she put him in a private school. At 36, she still lived with her son and shared a two-bedroom apartment with a co-worker. Michelle lived in the Green Springs Apartments in College Park at Roosevelt Highway and Green Springs Road. She worked from Monday through Friday. She got off work at 7:00 p.m. and regularly got home around 7:15 p.m. Michelle drove to work in a 2024 silver Toyota Corolla, insured by the Lawrence Jackson Insurance Agency. Lawrence came to the Green Springs Apartments to stalk Michelle twice and knew her whereabouts. One night, Lawrence went to the apartment complex around 7:10 p.m. and hid behind a trash bin in the parking lot where Michelle usually parked her car. The darkness started covering College Park at 7:15 p.m. when Michelle parked her silver Toyota Corolla and checked her phone for missed calls when Lawrence surged out of his hideout to reach her.

"Hi Michelle, how are you doing?" asked Lawrence with his handgun concealed on his thigh and his two hands in Latex Exam gloves.

"Fine, what are you doing here?" answered Michelle with the driver-side window down.

"Nothing. You're just back from work?" before Michelle could answer the question, Lawrence shot her at close range in the back of her neck, rolled up all the vehicle windows with his hands gloved, and locked the car doors. The victim agonized in her blood and died on the spot.

Lawrence went quickly to his car, parked three feet away from Michelle's car. He returned to his office on Riverdale

Road and called his wife to apologize for working late. He put the 9mm pistol back in the safe where he kept his insurance money before depositing it in the bank. Lawrence disposed of the Latex Exam gloves on his hands in the trash can in the bathroom of the insurance agency. He used the faucet water to wash his hair, clean his face, and drive home.

Brandon realized his mother was late coming home and took it upon himself to fix his diner. He cooked his favorite macaroni and cheese with fried chicken and watched TV all night. Around 10:30 p.m. that night, when he was about to go to bed, Brandon went to his mother's roommate, Victoria, to express his concern. Victoria called Michelle's phone, left a voice message, and texted. She urged the boy to go to bed while waiting for Michelle to call or text. Brendon didn't find his mother in bed when he woke up the following day. He then left the apartment to the parking lot and found his mother's 2024 Toyota Corolla parked in the designated spot. At his approach to the vehicle, he made a gruesome discovery. His mother was in the driver's seat, and her head was hanging on her chest. Brendon returned to the apartment to call Victoria, who came to consider the magnitude of the horrible scene. She called 911, and the police were dispatched within five minutes. The police barricaded the parking lot and proceeded to interview Brendon and Victoria. The ambulance was brought in, and the body was taken to the Grady Hospital after the investigation team gathered all the evidence. Brendon, at age 17, was devastated and couldn't cope with losing his dear mother. He tried to contact his father, who was living in New Jersey. Brendon had no other option but to move in with his father, who tried many times to get custody of the boy. The battle with Michelle wasn't easy, and the court granted her complete custody of boy. Brandon's father, Henry Lyle, moved on with his life, married another woman, and had two girls. Brandon had never met his two siblings and probably had no choice but to live with them. His father was devastated by the situation but started to plan for Brandon to join the family. The police investigation team didn't waste time going after the perpetrator of Michelle's murder. The day after the murder, two detectives went to Michelle's job to interview her bosses and co-workers who worked closely with her. To the question of who could want the death of the Walmart assistant manager, the name of a former lover surfaced. Manuel Somoza was Michelle's former lover who couldn't get over the breakout. He lived in College Park and would pop in her life occasionally, but Michelle didn't want anything to do with him. Somoza was a person who wouldn't take no for an answer and had anger and temper issues. He wasn't new in the Georgia justice system. When he was young, he was incarcerated many times, and the police didn't take long to get his address. Two detectives knocked at his door as soon as Somoza returned from work. He worked for a delivery company in Lithonia. He had an alibi, but the police couldn't pinpoint when the murder occurred. Manuel Somoza made gruesome accusations about a couple of Michelle's managers who were having affairs with her and offered her the assistant manager's position. Somoza's depositions made the investigation more complex. The next day, the two detectives went to Manuel Somaza's job to verify his alibis. His alibis stood off, for he was at work when the Michelle murder occurred. Then the detectives returned to Michelle's workplace to further interrogate the two managers. Somoza pointed out in his declaration that the two managers might have a reason for Michelle's death. After two months of investigation, the case went cold.

Two days after the murder, Lawrence Jackson pulled Michelle's insurance policy out of the file cabinet to find all the phone numbers on the contract list. He called Michelle's phone number, and her son Brendon answered.

"Hello," answered Brendon when her mother's phone rang.

"Hi, can I please talk to Michelle?" the voice said.

"She isn't here," Brendon replied.

"Where is she? I need to talk with her," the voice insisted.

"She is dead. She has been found dead in her can. Someone shoots her in the neck and leaves her body in her car," Brendon explained as coolly as possible.

"At what hospital is the body held? Is an autopsy done on the body to find the real cause of death?" the voice showed earnest concern.

"The body is currently at the Grady Hospital, and the autopsy is done, I think," Brendon answered the questions.

"Are there any funeral arrangements?" the voice continued.

"Michelle's mother is flying from Orange County, California, to find a funeral home for the burial," Brendon replied.

"What about you? Are you going to live with your grandmother in California?" the voice suggested.

"No, my father will send me a plane ticket to come and live with him in Newark, New Jersey," Brendon cheerfully added. The idea came to his mind to ask whom he was talking to, but the person on the other end hung up.

After the phone conversation, Lawrence called the Grady Hospital to request that Michelle's death certificate be emailed to him. Before noon, the death certificate was emailed to the Lawrence Jackson Insurance Agency. Then Lawrence called the Infinity Insurance Company in Irvin, Texas, to report a loss. He then faxed the death certificate and the claim form to request the death benefit of $50,000 paid to the Lawrence Jackson Insurance Agency. Without a hesitation the Infinity Insurance Company granted Lawrence's request.

Chapter 6

Big money started coming in.

Lawrence was very happy after negotiating with the Infinity Insurance Company and ordered pizza for his agency. Brenda Morales and Lawrence ate pizza all day, and their customers took some home. His agency was doing very well, and he was writing, on average, fourteen auto insurance a week. He made it available for the customers to pay a premium, endorse a policy, and file claims online. Lawrence left work around 5:30 p.m. and went home with great joy to an unexpected letter Bernice handed him as soon as he entered the house. It was a very lengthy letter. It read like this:

Dear Lawrence Jackson,

This letter is not a solicitation letter, and it's not sent to anybody. After careful study, we have decided to send you this letter. We're the secret group in America. We have studied your star in the sky and seen a bright future ahead of you. Your principal star has shifted from a dark stage to a sparkly bright star. A further study shows that there is some money heading your way. If you belong to our confrere, we can protect you and all your access. So, we're offering you a free-of-charge adhesion to our Secret Group. We'll help you and protect you.

Our group is a peaceful society where all members work hand in hand, and no one is left alone. We do everything as a group. We can make you an influential personality and a great manager in some companies we associate with. Some great characters you see on TV belong to our group. They work for us. We can do the same thing for you. We have many abilities that help us live fulfilling lives. We'll teach you how to make any woman love you. We'll teach you how to move back and forth from the physical realm to the spiritual realm. We'll mentor you to get the best out of our group until you get to the top of your life. You'll control who comes into your life and who goes out. You'll be able to enjoy life to the fullness of your ability. You'll enjoy many days on vacation with your family. We'll be there for you if you have an issue with the court system. We'll be there for you if you need help with the police. We'll be there for you if you need help with the government. It's a win-win situation. You'll never regret it. The opportunities in our group mount to the sky, and they're vast and immutable. Just sign the bottom of this letter, insert it in the envelope provided, and mail it back to us, and we'll take care of the rest.

Best Regards
The Secret Group

When Lawrence finished reading the letter, he raised his head to look up at his wife, standing before him while he was reading the letter. Lawrence had a horrified look on his face as if something were wrong.

"What's it?" Bernice asked.

"Sit down and read for yourself," Lawrence replied, handing the letter to his wife. She took the note and sat down next to him.

"Who're these people?" she asked after reading the letter.

"I don't know. How do they have my name?" he asked.

"Maybe you have ordered office supplies from a secret society without knowing," she affirmed.

"No, I haven't ordered supplies from any secret society," he insisted.

"We shouldn't let this letter resides in this house," she said.

"What should we do?" he asked with a trembling voice.

"We should destroy it and throw the garbage outside," she proposed.

"Joshua .... " She called her son in a loud voice.

"Mommy," answered the boy from the bedroom. He walked to the living where his two parents were sitting, a look of anguish on their faces.

"Go to the kitchen and bring me a pair of scissors," his mother commanded.

"Here are the scissors" the boy handed her the pair of scissors.

"Please don't get involved with these people," she said to his husband while cutting the letter and the two envelopes that came with it.

"I don't know them, and I don't know how they have gotten my name," he said.

"These people will promise to help you, but instead, they will destroy," she added while raping apart everything that came with the letter. She put all the little pieces of paper in the kitchen trash can, removed the plastic bag from the trash can, and threw it in the garbage bin outside. She came back in and set up the dining table for the family. They all ate and went respectively to their favorite electronic gadget. Bernice went to the new TV set, Lawrence grabbed his laptop, Joshua retrieved his new tablet, and Grace her new Apple phone. Lawrence made many changes to his two-bedroom apartment. He replaced his old analog TV with a smart one glued to the wall, which Bernice loved to watch whenever at home. Finally, the kitchen saw new appliances replacing the old ones. Finally, there was a new microwave, blender, toaster, and air fryer.

Two weeks after the death of Michelle Cornett, Lawrence received at his office from the Infinity Insurance Company a check for $50,000. After depositing it at the Wells Fargo bank, he was thrilled to see the amount transferred to his bank account. Lawrence called his wife from work to ask her to set an appointment with her parents the following Sunday after church. Bernice immediately called her father and mother to tell them they would pay half the money owed the next Sunday. Her mother was overwhelmed because it was a little over three months when Lawrence acquired the loan. She couldn't believe it and felt joy mingled with doubt. She called Bernice's siblings to brag about Lawrence Jackson. She spent hours on the phone talking about how genuine and competent Lawrence was and how lucky Bernice was to find such a wonderful and humble man. She printed online the recipe of all the dishes she would make for the Jacksons.

Andrew and Liz were going to receive them as celebrities because Liz didn't consent to the fact that Andrew co-signed for the loan. It was a significant relief for her to learn that Lawrence was ready to pay half the loan back.

The same day, Lawrence went through his file cabinet and the files he had built for all his customers' contracts, on which he slid a life policy. He came across a file that got his attention. It was the file of Mrs. Katie Menefee. This customer of his was a perfect candidate for his scheme. Lawrence had collected Mrs. Menefee's whereabouts from the morning to the evening from Monday to Friday and on the weekends. He knew when she would be at work and when she would be at home. So, he got all her contacts at the end of the file. Lawrence made up his schedule to stalk Mrs. Menefee to know precisely when and where he could make a move on her.

Mrs. Menefee was a married woman who lived with her husband, Gerald Menefee. The couple was in their retirement years. Katie Menefee was an Assistant Principal at the Camp Creek Middle School, where the Fulton County Public School was preparing to celebrate her last days with the school system. She was well known in College Park, and all her students adored her because of her unique relationship with the parents of her students. Students and faculty celebrated her on different occasions throughout the academic year. The Fulton School District gave her an advance of a lump sum of money toward her retirement. Mrs. Menefee used the cash to purchase a brand-new electric car Tesla X300 that Lawrence had insured for her. She had full coverage of the vehicle. Mrs. Menefee had two sons who were adults and were in the USA Army and traveled around the world all the time. Mrs. Menefee lived with her husband Gerald, who retired from the CSX railway company a year earlier. Gerald and Katie Menefee had only one vehicle, the 2024 white Tesla X300, that they utilized for errands and personal business. Mrs. Menefee loved this car; that was so dependable compared to her former vehicles and helped her avoid wasting time trying to fill a tank while on her way to Camp Creek Middle. Gerald always waited until Katie returned from work before he could go grocery shopping. They were inseparable, married for forty-two years, and had two children and many grandchildren who occasionally visited them.

Liz Dove woke up early to cook different dishes for the Jackson family, whom they were expecting around 3:00 p.m. after church. She gave much consideration to this visit of the Jackson family. Liz loved to cook, and Andrew helped a little in the kitchen, but this visit differed from previous visits. This visit was a sign for Lawrence to prove what he could do to the in-laws. The in-laws had never considered him for a long time because he was a broke man and had difficulty taking good care of his family. Bernice had called her father to beg for money for milk and groceries for Joshua and Grace, her two children. Liz and Andrew had prepared the table on the appointment day before Lawrence, his wife, and the two children arrived in their old Ford Taurus. The Doves invited two other families from the church for a luncheon. A long table was set up from the chicken to the dining room and covered with white linen, and many chairs were neatly arranged around the table. In the center of the table were fruits like grapes, oranges, apples, mango, banana, and pineapple in a crystal glass plate. On the side of the fruits were steak, fried fish, shrimp, and lobster dishes. A large stack of white napkins folded into two was at the table's edges next to the silverwares. On the other side of each plate, Liz put a bottle of orange juice and a bottle of non-alcoholic champagne. The setting looked like a banquet for a wealthy prince. Andrew and Liz presented their church friends to Lawrence before they all started eating and drinking for the rest of the evening. After a good time together, Lawrence handed Andrew a check of $25,000 to take to the bank the next day to honor his engagement to the bank of America.

Chapter 7

Mrs. Katie Menefee's death

This Monday morning wasn't a usual morning for Lawrence. He woke up early, took a warm shower, and dressed up for work. His wife wanted to know the reason for the early morning work. His alibi was he had more duties and more responsibilities to take care of. At 6:00 a.m., he drove off from his house to Mrs. Menefee's apartment complex to stalk his new victim. He parked his Ford Taurus three feet away from Mrs. Menefee's white Tesla X300 and monitored who was leaving Menefee's building. Sharply at 6:30 a.m. Mrs. Menefee went down the stairs of her building, quickly jumped in her car, and drove off. After she left, Lawrence stayed behind to observe and study Mrs. Menefee's environment. She lived on the second floor of building 802 of the complex, and her car was parked adjacent to the building, at the end of which was a large garbage bin to collect the trash. Building 802 was the last one on the far end of the apartment complex, ten feet away from the iron fence. Before jumping into his car, Lawrence walked around the fence to familiarize himself with the area. He went to work and conducted business as usual. Brenda Morales was shocked when she came to see her boss at work before her, and she tried to find out why Lawrence came in so early. But Lawrence wouldn't give her a valid reason, so the girl brushed it off and jumped on her daily routine. Lawrence left work early to go home and left the rest of his responsibilities in the hands of Branda. When he got home around 3:00 p.m., another letter from the secret group was waiting for him. His wife greeted him as he walked into the apartment, squinting at him while handing him the letter. He grabbed it and dropped himself on the living room couch. The letter read:

Dear Lawrence Jackson,

We're sending you this letter after careful consideration and study. It's not a random selection letter. We don't send this letter just to anyone, but we send it to peculiar people. We have studied your star and are thrilled about what we have found on you. We saw that your star had shifted from the peripheral cosmos layer to the upper layer. That shift was that you have some financial breakthroughs on the horizon. Therefore, we're sending you this invitation letter to join our club for your complete protection from any adversities you'll encounter in the future. We've people working for us in any domain of life you'll find yourself in. We've already assigned a mentor to teach you what to do in every situation. We'll follow you until you're fully evolved. Many influential people you see on TV, in courthouses, or in hospitals across the nation work for us and defend our causes. In every issue, you need to know the sign to know who is on your side and who isn't. We'll protect you and your family and anything that belongs to you. We have an initiation session coming up soon, and we hope you can participate in this unforgettable event. Please sign the bottom of this page and return it to us. We'll do the rest to enroll you in our secret world. You'll not regret it, and it'll be the best decision.

Sincerely
The Team

After reading the letter, Lawrence handed it to his wife to read. Bernice looked more perplexed after reading the letter and was speechless for a long while. Then her husband broke the silence:

"What do you think we should do?"

"I don't know."

"Do you want us to join the cult?".

"Noh, these people cause more harm than good."

"What do we do with the letter?"

"We'll tear it like the other time."

"What do we do to stop the letter from coming?".

"I don't know."

"Do you want us to report this to the police?".

"They don't commit a crime by soliciting our adhesion in their group. I'm going to destroy the letter each time it comes in. That'll do it".

On that note, Bernice stood up and walked to the kitchen, where she grabbed a pair of scissors to cut the letter into pieces. Then, she went out to dump the small pieces of the letter into the trash bin. When she returned, Bernice went to the kitchen to finish cooking the dish she was making before her husband came home. She set the dining table, and the whole family ate and chatted. Then Lawrence took his wife and the two children to Lenox Square, the Atlanta Mall, to buy clothes and shoes for the entire family. Lenox Square was a massive mall with many different department stores and was full of activities when they got there. The mall was just thirty minutes' drive away from their residence. They spent the entire evening at the mall buying nice and expensive clothes, jewelry, and shoes for everyone in the family. They also purchased food from many vendors in the food courtyard, and together, they ate, holding their shopping bags in their hands. They had a blast and a good time together until the mall closed at 9:00 p.m. when they got into their car to drive home. Bernice managed to get two designer dresses for the Saturday getaway Lawrence was planning since he collected the death benefits. Lawrence spent a little over $1,500 that evening on behalf of his family, and they all came home tired and satisfied. It was the first time they enjoyed the company of each other since money was the stumbling block and the handicap. Bernice suggested that Lawrence buy a new car and move from the two-bedroom apartment to a new house. Lawrence rejected all that financial entanglement at this point of his life. He would consider a new car and house whenever he was on the road to financial independence. He was so concerned about the loan he got from the Bank of America and would do anything to pay it off first. After the loan was paid off, he would consider doing anything valuable for himself and for his family. Lawrence desired to buy two cars, one Porch for the weekends and a Tesla electric car for work. Besides, he would consider a new two-car garage house in an expensive neighborhood in Atlanta. Every night he saw himself in a dream living large, having everything he needed within his reach. Lawrence promised himself to do anything to reach his goal and removed every handicap from his trajectory to a financial success.

Three days later, Lawrence woke up early morning to prepare for work. He took a warm shower, made a hot coffee, and put on his home clothes. He carried his work clothes in a plastic bag. He drove to work and entered his office to retrieve two Latex gloves and his 9 mm pistol, fully loaded. Then he drove to Mrs. Menefee's apartment complex and parked his car three feet away from building 802 at 6:15 a.m. after he locked the safe. Mrs. Menefee walked down the stairs of her building with her Fulton County laptop bag strap around her shoulder and a file folder in her left hand. She opened the back door and dropped the laptop bag and the file folder. Lawrence approached her when she opened the driver's side door and started a conversation.

"Good morning, Mrs. Menefee, how are you doing?".

"Fine, and you?".

"I'm doing well, thanks."

"What are you doing here this early?". Mrs. Menefee got into the driver's seat.

"Oh, I'm here to meet a client." Lawrence held the driver-side door with his left hand and tightened his right hand on his pistol. Mrs. Menefee pulled down the seat belt and rotated her body forty-five degrees to buckle up when Lawrence shot her in the back of the neck, at close range. The lady crumbled in her seat, and Lawrence readjusted the body in the car seat, locked all the vehicle doors properly, and strolled gently to his car. Then, he drove to his office to remove the gloves, the handgun, and home clothes. He discarded the gloves on his hands and put his gun in the safe after reloading it with ammunition. He cleaned himself up in the insurance agency's bathroom and wore clean office clothes. Lawrence went to the office file cabinet to retrieve Mrs. Menefee's file and moved it to the section where he put Michelle Cornett's information around 9:00 a.m. Brenda Morales came in to open the agency, she was stunned to see the door open. She saw her boss working on the phone and organizing the file cabinet. She couldn't ask him a question but jumped into cleaning the office and rearranging the waiting room seats.

Around 10:30 a.m., Mr. Gerald Menefee came down the building 802 to dump the trash, and he realized that his wife's Tesla X300 was still in the parking lot. He walked to the car and couldn't believe what he saw. He dropped the trash bag on the ground and tried to open the car doors. After several unsuccessful attempts to get in the car, Gerald returned to the apartment and called the police. He called 911 and described what he saw to the emergency dispatcher when many police cars rushed to the scene. Gerald couldn't make a full and vivid description of the body of his wife in the car because the car windows were tinted black, making it difficult to see inside. The police barricaded the parking lot next to building 802 with a yellow ribbon, making it impossible for anyone to get out or get in the parking lot. The police forced the back door of the vehicle to be able to open the car doors and get to the body. A crime scene examination team came in a white van with all equipment and all elements of the crime scene. The team searched for the fingerprints of the perpetrator but realized the criminal had gloves on. Chief Detective

Mark Brown from the Atlanta division coordinated the effort to preserve the evidence and the story the crime scene was telling. Gerald cried hysterically and couldn't approach his wife's body transported in an ambulance to the Grady Hospital for an autopsy. Detective Mark Brown took Gerald to his apartment to ask questions about his relationship with his wife. He requested Gerald to hand over the financial documents of the couple, bank documents, insurance policies, and car notes. He noticed that the couple had many credit card debts that could be a cause of the death, Mark Brown thought in the back of his head. He came down to the first floor and knocked on two doors to ask if anybody had heard a gunshot this morning from the parking lot. No one could confirm hearing anything; Mark Brown proceeded to check around and inside the trash bin against the fence at the end of the parking lot where the crime occurred. He then went to the apartment manager to request a camera recording of all the tenants' incoming and outgoing. Unfortunately, there was only one camera in the management office to monitor the transactions between office managers and the tenants. Mark Brown had a little to work with. The next day he went to the Camp Creek Middle School to talk with the school principal to find out if there could be a possible Mrs. Menefee's co-worker behind the assistant principal's death. The principal was devastated to learn the previous day about the tragic death of the beloved assistant principal. Her husband, Gerald, had called to break the bad news, and the school personnel and faculties were grieving the loss of Mrs. Menefee. They couldn't understand that anyone on earth would want the sweet assistant principal dead, who was so outgoing with a helping heart, to embrace anyone on her path. The emotions and the grieves in Camp Creek Middle

School were unbearable for the detective, who left the school quickly for the Grady Hospital to collect the bullet that killed Mrs. Menefee for testing. He sent the bullet to the FBI's state of art crime lab facility in Quantico, Virginia, to compare with Mrs. Michelle Cornett's bullet fragment last month. The two murders were about a month apart and might be related because of the close vicinity. After a week of testing, the FBI found that the bullets that killed Michelle Cornett and Mrs. Menefee were a perfect match and came from the same handgun barrel. FBI got involved in Mrs. Menefee's case and requested a meeting with the Atlanta police chief and Mark Brown to elaborate a procedure to find a serial killer on the loose in College Park. It was decided that the police chief call the news outlets for a conference to inform all the inhabitants of College Park of a serial killer who targeted vulnerable females in parking lots. The conference caused panic among women seeking to enroll in self-defense classes to prepare for any attack from the supposed serial killer.

Two days after the death of Mrs. Menefee, Lawrence called her from his office phone, but the call went to voice mail, and he didn't want to leave any messages. Then he called her husband, who answered the phone:

"Hello!"

"Can I talk to Mrs. Menefee, your wife?"

"Why?"

"I call her phone, and she doesn't answer."

"Who're you?"

"I'm the insurance agent, Lawrence Jackson, on Riverdale Road. Do you remember now?".

"I remember you; payment isn't due yet. So why you're calling?"

"I have found a discount for her car that she can qualify for. Her Tesla car's safety feature can bring her monthly premium down about five dollars."

"What safety feature is that?"

"It's an antitheft feature inside the car that makes it retraceable anywhere."

"Is this new to you?"

"Is your wife around, or can you send her to come in and sign for the discount."

"She isn't here."

"Where is she?"

"She got shot three days ago."

"Who can do a horrible thing like that?"

"I don't know?"

"Is the autopsy result out yet?"

"The hospital is working on that, and I don't know how long it'll take."

"What hospital is her body taken to?"

"Grady Hospital in Atlanta."

"Normally, it takes two days for Grady Hospital to develop the autopsy result."

"It's been three days now, and I don't know what to do."

"I'm so sorry for your loss, and my condolences to you and your family."

Lawrence Jackson hung up the phone and went to the file cabinet to find the telephone of the Grady Hospital to inquire about Mrs. Menefee's death certificate. He called the mortuary at Grady Hospital to have Mrs. Menefee's death certificate emailed to his agency's electronic address. Within thirty minutes, the death certificate was emailed to him, and he called Texas, the Infinity Insurance Company he worked with, to report a client's death. Lawrence printed the death certificate and faxed a claim form to Infinity Insurance Company. Lawrence happily ordered pizza for his employee and customers in the waiting room. He said this would be the last time he had taken a person's life. He promised to use the upcoming money wisely and never have to utilize the gun for the money. From childhood to adulthood, being poor all his life was hard. Then his life with his mother paraded through his mind. Tears started coming down his cheek that he couldn't control because it was the most painful moment of his life. His father left him early, and his mother couldn't handle the family alone.

Before the day's end, Lawrence called to the back office, Brenda, to inform her that the insurance agency would be closed on Saturdays and Sundays. Brenda should advise the weekend customers to make payments and endorsements online. Lawrence had a big plan for the weekend for him and his wife to dine in a fancy restaurant in Savanah, Georgia. The Casa Marina Restaurant was a famous restaurant in Savanah where many celebrities and state officials came to eat and have fun. Lawrence had heard about this restaurant since he was a little boy. It was a restaurant right at the beach where many vital figures would come to enjoy themselves. The restaurant had a playground next to it for children of all ages.

Chapter 8

Jackson family in turmoil

The following Saturday, Lawrence arranged for a babysitter who lived in their apartment complex to watch his two children. He paid $200 for the day to care for his children so he could have time alone with his wife to give her the total attention she had long craved. He rented a golden Cadillac Escalator from the Enterprise Car Rental in College Park for the occasion. Early in the morning, Bernice called in a longtime friend, a hairdresser, to do her lovely hair while Lawrence was scheduling to book a table at the restaurant in Savannah, Georgia, and the car. The restaurant was prevalent in South Georgia, where many wealthy people would come and eat, with a gorgeous ocean view. Bernice's transformation for the occasion was breathtaking. She looked like Marilyn Monroe in the designer dress and shoes she recently purchased from Lenox Square for the event. Lawrence could never believe his wife's beauty, which he ceased to admire when financial burdens were pounding on his shoulders. He couldn't stop complimenting his wife on their way to Savannah, which evolved the pride of womanhood she lost shortly after giving birth to her first child. They took the I-75 South from Riverdale Road, heading South of

Georgia, and then got on the I-16 East to Savannah, Georgia. They arrived thirty minutes early and decided to spend a frolicking moment on the ocean shore. They left the Cadillac Escalator to walk closer to the seashore, where many people were having fun under a blue, cerulean sky. Some people were swimming; others sat on the beautiful white crystal sand that neatly displayed the coastal line and the sea. The immensity of the sea and the beautiful sky seemed to collide at the far end of this magnificent spectacle. Bernice, who was walking with her husband, was overwhelmed with friction because this was the first time, she had visited a beach in her lifetime. She felt the grittiness of the sand beneath her feet, causing her to cling to her husband, who was strolling along the seashore. The sun's blistering rays made her squint through some ladies who lay flat on the never-ending shore to bathe in the sunlight to absorb the sun's rays. The sounds of the majestic ocean and the numerous waves crashing down to the coast sent an evening air that tingled Bernice's nostrils. The salty air cooled her face, making her feel like a seagull in this astonishing atmosphere. The feeling of belonging overcame her; she came closer to some ladies sitting in comfy chairs admiring the stunning scenery. The whole environment was causing her to breathe more rapidly and intensely than usual, like a different species in the marine world. Bernice could see a couple of floating yachts from a far distance waiting to take the journey or voyage over the sea. She thought that they could ship by night one day. Sooner or later, her husband would be financially independent to get whatever her family wanted to acquire, her mind said. She turned to Lawrence, who was enjoying the moment within himself, asking him:

"Hey, Lawrence, why have we never been to the beach?"

"I don't know, but now we can come as much as possible."

Lawrence looked at his watch and realized they had a few minutes left to go to the restaurant. Their appointment was at 5:00 p.m., and they didn't want to be late, for the restaurant was very strict about the timing. The Casa Marina restaurant was a big boat reorganized for a spectacular dining experience that accommodated state senators, government officials, and politicians. It offered international cousins at five-star levels, making wealthy people come with their families and friends. A glass door led to a lobby where a young lady checked all the guests in with a smile. Then, as Lawrence and Bernice pulled the glass door to enter the restaurant, a soft female voice welcomed them.

"Hello, do you all have a reservation for the evening?" the voice asked.

"Yes, we do," answered Lawrence.

"What's your name, sir?" the lady added.

"My name is Mr. Lawrence Jackson," Lawrence replied.

"Oh! I see your reservation at 5:00 p. m. "the lady had a tablet on the desk in front of her and beckoned another waitress in a suit and tie to lead the couple to the assigned table for two.

The place was lovely and incredibly organized. All the waiters and waitresses wore white uniforms with a tablet in each one's hands to get the accuracy of what the guest wanted. Light everywhere in the restaurant sent brightened rays on the shining woodwork all over the interior. The interior was magnificently decorated with pictures of celebrities who came to easy in Casa Marina. The edge of the tables was gold, reflecting the brightness of the restaurant's ceiling lights in different directions. A peaceful piano melody from Beethoven's classical pieces was faintly playing in the background, making it seem like it was coming from afar. The alluring aroma flowed through the restaurant to prepare the guests' stomachs for the succulent meal they were expecting. Lawrence Jackson's waitress brought a silver plate of appetizers, which smell covered them with an intermingling scent of salad, garlic loaves of bread, dry tortilla, and butter. A plate of steak, shrimp, and lobsters was laid before Lawrence and Bernice while another waitress unveiled everything that came with the appetizer plate. The couple was devouring the steak, shrimp, and lobster when someone approached their table with a note to move to the initiation curtain on the far right of the restaurant. Lawrence was perplexed and didn't understand what the man in the black suit insinuated. There was a kind of argument between Lawrence and the man. His wife explained that they weren't there for any initiation but for quality time for husband and wife. She was quickly brushed off because she wasn't relevant to this matter that wholly rested upon his husband's shoulders. Amid this argument, two men from the curtain in the far right of the restaurant joined in the altercation. The two men wore black suits with a garment purse on their waists and a long golden chain descending to their bellies. The two men held an incensory full of blazing charcoals and without incense. There was a big silence in the restaurant, and people from different tables watched what was happening. The men claimed they sent two invitation letters to Lawrence for his initiation to the Secret Group of America, and Lawrence responded favorably to their call. Lawrence tried to explain to the men that he tore the two letters and threw them in the trash bin outside their apartment. The men insisted that tearing the letters wasn't an acceptable way to reject their invitation, and rather they should have burnt the letters, which would have returned to the sender as rejected. Lawrence said he didn't know what to do with the letters, and there were no instructions for discarding them. The two men dropped their incensory on the floor, grabbed Lawrence by the arms, and tried to carry him to the curtain. His wife, Bernice, tried to stop the men from carrying her husband away but was pushed away violently. That was when Lawrence realized the seriousness of what was happening and fought back. A fight broke out between Lawrence and the cult members, who could not subdue their victim. During the commotion, the blazing charcoals were burning the wooden floor of the restaurant. Another cult member threw a gallon of gasoline on the blazing incensory, and the restaurant caught fire. People started running toward the entrance of the restaurant, screaming. But the only glass door to the restaurant was locked. People successfully broke the glass door and ran out before the blazing fire caught up with them. Lawrence and Bernice managed to get out successfully and ran to their car parked in the rear of the restaurant. They jumped in the Cadillac Escalator and drove off to the I-16 West. Two cult members also jumped in a black Mercedes S400 to chase after the Jacksons. Lawrence was speeding, and the black Mercedes was right on his tail. The Mercedes caught up with the Cadillac and tried to push Lawrence off the road to a side ditch. The chase continued until Lawrence drove into Macon Police Station off I-75 North. Lawrence reported to the police that he and his wife were being chased by people they didn't know. When he came out to identify the perpetrators, the black Mercedes was nowhere to be found. Lawrence and Bernice were given paper and pen to report the incident separately so that the police could investigate the allegations. After the report, a police officer was assigned to escort the Jacksons to College Park. Bernice was still afraid and shaken from the ordeal and couldn't go to the babysitting apartment to bring her two children home. Lawrence went to the babysitter's apartment, two buildings away from their apartment. The two children, Joshua and Grace, were thrilled to see their father and mother, who had never left them with a stranger before in their lifetime. They came in to see their mother, who wasn't talking and was still shocked by what had happened to her in Savannah. Her emotion was so high that she couldn't believe she had hardly escaped a burning fire death. She couldn't cook or eat anything and took a shower and went to bed early, leaving the children in the care of her husband. The next day, Sunday, everything returned to normal; they regained their joy of living together, playing music, watching TV, cooking food, and playing games. The following Monday, Lawrence went to work and resumed his activities as usual. A week from the day he filed the claim against Mrs. Menefee's life insurance policy, a check for fifty thousand dollars came in. The Infinity Insurance Company also sent a receipt of the death benefit payment to the Insurance Commissioner's Office in Atlanta, Georgia, as it had in the previous case of Ms. Michelle Cornett. The insurance commissioner's office took two weeks to process the receipt due to the numerous correspondences from insurance companies operating in Georgia. The day the check came in, Lawrence was delighted with his accomplishment and performance for his agency's success. He ordered pizza and soft drinks for his employee and clients in the waiting room to celebrate with him. He went to his bank to deposit the full amount in his checking account with Wells Fargo Bank. When he returned to the office, Lawrence called his father-in-law to schedule a meeting with the loan officer Jimmy at Bank of America to pay off the balance. The following Wednesday at 9:00 a.m. Andrew and Lawrence met at the Bank of America parking lot in College Park to finalize the loan deal Andrew co-signed for Lawrence's insurance business. Liz came with her husband Andrew to witness this incredible event that she couldn't believe was real. They went in together and sat in the loan officer Jimmy's office to deliver a check for $25,500. The final balance on loan didn't accrue much interest because Lawrence managed to pay off the loan within six months of the deal date. After the closure of the loan account, Liz and Andrew wanted to visit their daughter Bernice who quitted going to her part-time grocery store job. She devoted all her time to housework and caring for her two children, ensuring their academic performance was up to the standard. Lawrence couldn't go home with his in-laws because he had to go and take care of the agency. The agency reported on average, fifteen new businesses and numerous weekly endorsements. Liz and Andrew spent time with Bernice, who had already sent her two children on the bus to College Park Elementary School. She wasn't expecting her parents that morning, but she went quickly to the kitchen to make a delicious breakfast. Bernice toasted some loaves of bread; she scrambled some eggs while cooking some sausages on the side. She made two plates for her mother and father sitting by the new dining set Lawrence purchased a week ago to replace the old one. Liz was very impressed with how the kitchen refrigerator was full of juices, vegetables, and fruits. Next to the refrigerator was a separate freezer of high-quality meats and fish. Liz got a gallon of orange juice and some apples from the refrigerator to complete her breakfast. The Doves ate and drank and chatted until they returned home to Cobb County in the early afternoon and were satisfied with the stable conditions in which their daughter was living with a loving husband and two young children. Lawrence came home around 6:30 p.m. to learn that Liz and Andrew spent quality time with their daughter and were satisfied with the Jackson family's living conditions. The apartment's new changes, such as furniture, computer desk, and dining set, impressed them. Lawrence was also happy but wouldn't express his emotions about lifestyle changes. That night Lawrence had a troubling dream which he didn't know if he should tell his wife or not. He saw that he had bought a new house with a big basement, and his two kids were playing in the living room. The dreamhouse had a well-maintained swimming pool in the front, but the house wasn't located in Georgia. It had a two-car garage leading to a vast kitchen and living room with pure leather furniture on a thick green carpet. He had a housemaid laundering his clothes and garments; his wife didn't look like Bernice. His wife in the dream was slim with different skin colors, and she was teaching the German langue to the kids in a strong tone of voice. He woke up around 3:15 a.m. and couldn't go back to sleep but thought about the dream the rest of the night to figure out the meaning. He knew many dreams were meaningless, but this one was so real that it might be relevant to his current situation. Lawrence was observing his wife when she was making him breakfast before he could go to work with hesitation in his mind. Finally, he decided not to talk about his dream of the previous night because it filled him with many unanswered questions. He convinced himself that the dream couldn't be close to reality because he loved his wife Bernice and had no need for a different spouse. He loved the house in the dream and wished it could be real. The house was massively built on a vast landscape with an iron fence, a huge metal gate, and different flowers. But why would his wife speak German to his two children, Joshua and Grace? Besides, the house wasn't in Georgia. Was it in a different state or a different country? He couldn't understand many elements of the dream and wished he could find someone to interpret all that. So, he tried to put the dream into his unconscious and forget about it. He tried hard to make the dream disappear from his memory, but it was so strong on his psychic all day.

70

Chapter 9

The FBI's involvement in the two cases

The Insurance Commissioner, Henry Wade, called a meeting with his staff after realizing two death payments to the same beneficiary within three months. The Commissioner exposed the two payment receipts from the Infinity Insurance Company sent from their headquarters in Texas. The payments were made back-to-back to the Lawrence Jackson insurance agency in College Park, Georgia, in less than three months. The office of the Commissioner evaluated the benefit payment receipts and called Infinity Insurance Company for a specific request. The Commissioner demanded that the policies of the late Mss. Michelle Cornett and Mrs. Menefee faxed to the Commissioner's office, and the original documents in the two cases were mailed to Mr. Wade's office. After a day of deliberations, the Commissioner's office suspected that insurance fraud, a federal crime, was committed and needed the involvement of a federal agency. Mr. Wade called the FBI headquarters in Atlanta to expose the situation and finally secured a meeting with Agent Frank Tucker and detective Mark Brown the following day. At 2:00 p.m., Mr. Henry Wade, Mr. Mark Brown, and Frank

Tucker met at the FBI headquarters on Flowers Road in Chamblee, Georgia. Commissioner Henry Wade brought all the insurance documents involved in the two cases to the meeting. In contrast, detective Mark Brown got the crime scene photos and the fragmented bullets collected at the autopsy room, with the bullet shells recovered from the victims' cars. The two men exposed their cases to the special agent Frank Tucker who was overwhelmed with the evidence against Lawrence Jackson's insurance agency. The two crimes had many similarities; both shots targeted the back of the victims' head with just one bullet. On the spot, the team decided to put Lawrence Jackson under surveillance, wiretap all his phones, and use the GPS to track all his movements and observe any meetings with suspected co-conspirators. The agent Frank Tucker went before a federal judge to present his case to request an active search warrant against the insurance agency. Mr. Tucker set up a team of agents who listened to Lawrence Jackson's phone conversations and monitored his movements. Lawrence's mobile phone, Bernice's cellphone, and the agency's analog landline phone were tapped, and every day an agent listened to all incoming and outgoing calls from these devices. Lawrence had no immediate friends to call, but his wife was constantly on the phone with her parents and two siblings for most of her time. Lawrence called mostly his customers from his office phone as a courtesy call to remind them of their upcoming premium payment. After a week of no significant lead, agent Frank Tucker sent a presumed auto insurance prospect with a hidden camera to purchase a policy. The potential was an undercover female agent who came in to buy a policy with Lawrence and recorded all the detail of the agency's practice. But nothing suspicious was reported.

A week later, Lawrence reviewed his clients' folders and found Jerome McDonnell's file containing all the client's daily activities. He realized that Jerome would be an easy target and changed his mind. Jerome was a seventy-two-year-old man living in an old brick single-family house on Buffington Road. Jerome's father owned the house and paid it off after his dad passed away when he was thirty-five years old. Jerome was on a fixed income with the Social Administration Department and shared the house with his son, who spent every weekend with his fiancée's family. The fiancée's family owned a big Maison on a three-hectare land in Fayette County, where Jerome's son helped the in-laws run a family business. Jerome was always vulnerable on the weekends when he had nobody to take him grocery shopping and cook his meals. Lawrence couldn't pass on this opportunity and wouldn't get involved in this new case that would bring him another $50,000. He told himself to hire a killer who would carry out his plan. He searched online for a credible assassin who could do a clean job that would leave no trail linking him to the crime. His search led him to a possible gang group in South Central Los Angeles, California, where some Mexican hitmen operated. Lawrence convinced himself that it would be good to visit Los Angeles to find a Mexican assassin who could get the job done properly, for he was willing to pay someone $5,000 to carry out his plan. Lawrence told his wife he would take a business trip to Los Angeles to meet a client at a dinner table for insurance purposes. He would leave the Hartsfield-Jackson International Airport in Atlanta on a Friday evening and return on Sunday. After receiving his wife's approval, Lawrence purchased online a plane ticket from Atlanta to LAX the following Friday. Bernice prepared her husband's suitcase and inserted his favorite suit and ties for business occasions. Lawrence came home early that Friday, and his wife dropped him at the airport to fly a business class to Los Angeles. Agent Frank Tucker was tipped that Lawrence was dropped off at the Hartsfield-Jackson International Airport. Agent Frank rushed to the airport and found Lawrence with just a small suitcase in line before the check-in desk of Delta Airlines. Agent Frank got in the queue until he approached the check-in desk to find out that the aircraft was leaving in one hour for LAX. He showed his FBI badge and purchased the plane ticket to Los Angeles with his eyes on the insurance agent's moves. Agent Frank called his wife to bring him a suitcase with his clothes and add different hats, wigs, and eyeglasses in the waiting hall. He wore many different outfits when following someone very close to disguise his appearance. Agent Frank's wife came to the entrance to deliver the suitcase when passengers boarded the Delta Airlines non-stop flight to LAX. An airport official accompanied her to the boarding door, and she hugged and kissed her husband, wishing him good luck on the assignment. Agent Frank took a seat in the rear of the Delta aircraft 787 while Lawrence was sitting in the middle, making it easy for the FBI agent to keep his eyes on him. The plane landed at the Los Angeles International airport around 6:30 p.m. pacific time, when darkness started taking over the beautiful cerulean, blue sky. Lawrence patiently grabbed his suitcase to exit the aircraft and went downstairs to call his wife. He was on the phone for about fifteen minutes while Agent Frank waited for him to see Lawrence's next move. After the phone calls, Lawrence stormed out of the Airport Hall and got in a taxicab waiting outside. Agent Frank also jumped in another taxi and ordered the driver to follow Lawrence's cab closely that was taking him to a Motel 6 on Central Avenue,

South Central Los Angeles. Frank changed his outfit and put a hat on before leaving his taxi and renting a room for the night at the Motel 6 rental office. He wanted a room that would face Lawrence's room to monitor all his movements and listen to telephone calls. Lawrence left his room to eat at McDonell, three blocks from Motel 6, because he was starving. Likewise, Agent Frank went to the same McDonell to order a chicken sandwich meal with large French fries and Pepsi. When both men returned to their respective rooms, Agent Frank called his GPS tracking team in Atlanta to instruct them to follow their suspect. The next day, around 10:00 a.m., Lawrence went to stand by the bus stop sign to catch a bus to downtown Los Angeles where he could find some homeless men who could help him in his search. Agent Frank put on a long wig and oversized sunglasses and came to the bus stop. Lawrence climbed the bus from the front to pay the fee while Agent Frank hopped on the bus through the rear door to sit on the back seat. Lawrence got off the bus in Downtown Los Angeles at the corner of Broadway Street and Eight Street. Agent Frank got off, too, after taking off his wig and the big sunglasses and putting on a blue Dodger cap with a reading glass. People's activities Downtown were up to the chart. Many people went on the sidewalks, peeping through glass windows displaying beautiful garments, suits, shoes, and much more.

Many jewelry stores, restaurants, shoe stores, clothing stores, handbag stores, banks, and different businesses operated along Broadway Street. People were going aimlessly up and down, bumping each other without knowing, and no one would ask, "why do you bump into me?". It was a part of the routine of busy weekends in Downtown Los Angeles, where many different cultures mingled to create a complex atmosphere. Agent Frank was scared he would lose track of the presumed suspect, who disappeared twice from the agent's eyes on the street. Lawrence went into a restaurant to buy something to eat, and Agent Frank was looking for him on the sidewalk until he immerged again on the street after eating his food. On the second occasion, Lawrence saw a food stand across the street selling different fruits ready to eat in plastic. He loved fruits and vegetables and couldn't resist the appeal of grapes, watermelon, mango, strawberry, pineapple, and apple in one place. He was walking slowly at the paste of the crowd until he saw a homeless man on a corner standing next to a shopping cart containing his dirty clothes. He approached the homeless man and asked where to find some Mexican hitmen in Los Angeles. The homeless man answered him harshly that he didn't know where to find such people. Agent Frank approached the man and gave him $10 to find out what Lawrence asked the homeless man. At the sight of $10, the man tried to hug Agent Frank because he was praying for just $5 to get something to eat, for he was starving. Agent Frank asked him the question the man in the blue shirt asked him. He replied that he wanted to know where to find a Mexican assassin in the city. When Agent Frank finished talking with the man, he saw Lawrence conversing with another homeless man across the street. After Lawrence left the man, Agent Frank approached him and offered him $20 to know the details of his conversation with the man in the blue shirt. The homeless man faithfully repeated his discussion with Lawrence, and Alvarado Park was the hangout place for such people, was his instruction. By the time Agent Frank gathered all information given to Lawrence, Frank saw him getting on a bus heading south of the city. It would take another thirty minutes for another bus going to Campton Bus Station via Alvarado Park would come. When they got to Alvarado Park, the bus driver made a hand signal to Lawrence to indicate that he was at the requested stop. He got off the bus, looking lost because the park was vast, and he didn't know where to start. So, he saw many people wandering in and out of the park. Some couples were walking and frolicking hand-in-hand in the garden, while others were chatting next to each other on benches. Across the street from the park were some stores busy with people purchasing various items they needed. There was a record store in the middle where Mexican music was coming out to cover the whole of Alvarado Park. In front of the music store, was a food stand where many people were standing to buy a stick of corn covered with mayonnaise and spicy seasoning. On the right side of this music store was a small grocery store where people came to purchase only Mexican food. Lawrence knew he was in the right place but didn't know whom to talk to. He decided to walk around the park to understand the activity better. He saw two Mexican guys standing at the park's edge, talking confidently. The two guys were about twenty-three years old, with heavy tattoos on their necks and arms. Lawrence went closer to them and greeted them amiably, but they didn't greet him back but instead asked him what he was up to. The two guys' faces weren't friendly, and he felt threatened when he admitted that he was looking for a hitman in Los Angeles for somebody who owed him money and refused to pay. One guy wrote a phone number on a piece of paper to call only at nighttime. The two guys continued their private conversation as if the request they had just received was standard. Lawrence was delighted he was on the right track and hoped to secure a good deal before returning to his wife and children. He found another bus that took him back to South Central, and he went back to his motel room to call his wife, who was dying from her husband's absence. As soon as Lawrence left Alvarado Park came Agent Frank looked for him for the whole afternoon but couldn't find him. He walked through and around the park several times and finally sat on a bench in Alvarado Park. He was starving and tired and angry at himself for losing sight of the man he came to spy on. However, a feeling of satisfaction went through him swiftly because he knew at least why Lawrence flew to Los Angeles, which was a great accomplishment. He took a cab back to the motel, saw the light in Lawrence's room, and heard him talking to his wife on his cell phone. Agent Frank called Delta Airlines to schedule a flight back to Hartfield-Jackson International Airport of Atlanta George the following day.

At exactly 9:00 p.m., Lawrence called the number that was given to him in Alvarado Park, and a man with a deep voice answered the phone:

"Hey, what's up?"

"Hey, my name is Lawrence. I got your number today in Alvarado Park".

"You talked with two of my guys early today?"

"Listen, meet me at the bus stop of Alvarado Park tonight at 10:00 p.m.".

"What's your name?".

"They call me Chollo."

"But, it's too late; we meet tomorrow morning?".

"You want to come or not? I work at night only."

"Yes, I'm coming."

"At 10:00 p.m. exact by the bus stop".

"Ok, see you there at 10:00 p.m.".

Chollo hung up the phone, and Lawrence held his cell phone by his left ear, thinking deeply about what he had just put himself into. Alvarado Park didn't look safe at night when there wasn't enough light. He took his courage with two hands, saying that he had come too far to turn around and needed to close this deal with Chollo before returning home. Lawrence called a UBER to schedule a round trip to Alvarado Park by 10:00 p.m., which arrived on time and dropped him by the bus stop at Alvarado Park. Chollo was there before him and went straight to the compensational aspect of the deal to see if it was worth the trouble. Lawrence laid down the plan to fly Chollo to Georgia the following Thursday and would collect the initial payment of $2,000. Lawrence promised to provide the accommodation until the execution of Jerome was accomplished, and Chollo would receive the rest of his money, $3,000. Chollo wrote his real name, Ruben Morales, on a paper he handed to his interlocutor and walked into the darkness. Lawrence walked to the UBER driver, who was waiting for him impatiently, and Lawrence promised to add a $5 tip to his fare to bring back a smile on his face.

Chapter 10

An imminent downfall

Monday morning, Agent Frank gathered all his collaborators to review the findings and exploited different options he had to take the case to a happy ending. All the agents involved in the case were convinced that Lawrence was behind the murder of Michelle Cornett and Mrs. Menefee. Some of the team members suggested waiting until they could catch Lawrence red-handed. On the other hand, Agent Frank wouldn't take the chance to risk the life of any resident of College Park. They took another step to monitor Lawrence's bank account activities to understand how he used his money. They took the case further to find a federal judge to request a search warrant for Lawrence's home and business office. Agent Frank gathered all the evidence to meet with a well-known judge, his friend, in the Atlanta federal courthouse. The judge granted him the search warrant to move smoothly through the Lawrence Jackson Insurance Agency business documents. With the search warrant documents under his hands, Agent Frank called the College Park Police station to bring in Lawrence Jackson for questioning in the death of Michelle Cornett and Mrs. Menefee since these victims were his clients at the time of their death. Lawrence was at work when the call came to ask him to go to the police station for a routine questioning regarding the killing of some of his insurance business acquaintances. He wanted to know why the police turned their attention to him five months after Michelle's tragic death. He was assured that it was routine questioning for anyone that had a connection to the victims before the day of their death. He didn't want to argue too much on the phone but agreed to be at the police station at 9:00 a. m. the following day. Lawrence became very perplexed after hanging up with the policeman on the other end, and many thoughts were going through his mind. He didn't know what the police knew about the two victims and what questions he would have to answer. He took his courage with two hands and was willing to meet with the College Park police. He continued to conduct business as usual and acted as if nothing significant had happened. Lawrence had never wanted to bring his business problem home to his wife because he loved to keep his business personality to himself. Lawrence, as a businessman, was utterly different from the family man his wife and children knew. When he got home that evening, he was greeted by a chihuahua dog that her children were asking for. It turned out that Bernice went to the store and purchased the chihuahua dog for the children. It was a beautiful dog that the whole family loved and enjoyed playing with. The new dog brought additional joy to the Jackson family, who cared for the dog. Bernice promised to take the dog for a daily walk, and Lawrence was appointed to buy the dog food every weekend. Lawrence forgot the pressure at work and went to bed with joy and laughter. He woke up in the middle of the night, around 3:15 a.m., to realize he had the same dream about a new expensive house he was living in with his family.

In the dream, he had a big home with a basement and his two kids playing in the living room. The dreamhouse had a swimming pool well maintained in the front yard, but the house wasn't located in Georgia. It had a two-car garage leading to a vast kitchen and living room with pure leather furniture on a thick green carpet. He had a housemaid laundering his clothes and garments; his wife didn't look like Bernice. His wife in the dream was slim with different skin colors and tones of voice. He wanted to wake up his wife, but she was sound asleep. He felt he needed to talk to somebody about this dream that kept coming to him, but he didn't know whom to turn to. He thought about his father, Robert, but no father figure existed. He felt the urge to look after his brother Mike, whom he hadn't spoken to for many years. His sister Laura wasn't an option because she wouldn't understand all he was going through with his career and family. He thought about finding a spiritual leader but wasn't a churchgoer and wouldn't fit in a church setting. Lawrence woke up early to shower and eat the typical breakfast his wife had made for him. He kissed his wife goodbye, knowing the considerable uncertainty before him with the appointment at the police station. He drove to College Park Police Station parking lot, sitting in his car thinking about what to say and what not to say. At 9:00 a.m., he reported to the police station and sat in the lobby, waiting for his turn to be called in. Fifteen minutes later, a police investigator took him to a room for a one-on-one conversation. The room was small, with a table in the middle and two chairs facing one another. The room windows were glass where people could see from the outside, but you couldn't see them from the inside. The ceiling was embedded with hidden cameras and speakers that could capture every movement and utterance. The interview was about the whereabouts of Lawrence in the days of the murder of Michelle Cornett and Mrs. Menefee. It was very casual, without any pressure to make Lawrence believe he was the prime suspect in the murder of the two victims. He accepted to give a saliva sample for a DNA test and a fingerprint to clear his name. He was released thinking he could get away with murder. On the other hand, as soon as Brenda Morales opened the doors to the Lawrence Jackson Insurance Agency, Agent Frank and his co-worker Agent Bryan presented her with a search warrant document. Agent Frank and Bryan went through the agency's file cabinet, looking for Michelle Cornett and Mrs. Menefee's files for a possible clue to help them crack the case. They found these files in a separate cabinet section with specific record-keeping data inside the folders. They found a safe they felt compelled to look through in Lawrence's back office but didn't have the combination numbers. Agent Frank called the police station to get the safe combination from Lawrence while he was on the line. Lawrence gave a combination number to the investigator interviewing him, thinking he would clean that safe as soon as he would get to his office. He didn't know that two FBI agents were going through all his belongings. Agent Frank and Bryan found a nine-millimeter handgun, a cache of ammunition, and a box of Latex gloves in the safe, which they took with them. With the findings, they drove to the Atlanta Hartfield-Jackson International Airport to book a special plane to Dulles International Airport. From the Dulles airport, the two agents drove to the FBI's state of art crime lab facility in Quantico, Virginia, to test the fingerprints on the handgun and the bullets. At the facility, the two agents took the handgun in their possession for fingerprint testing, where they found that only Lawrence Jackson's fingerprints were present. No other individual had used the handgun, and there was no trace of any other suspect. Then they went up to the gun unit, where they compared the two bullets that killed the two victims in Lawrence's case. The gun unit was a specialized piece of equipment made of solid iron, with the interior covered with a white rubber about 20 mm thick. The equipment was like a big tank with a cover that measured 8 feet long and about 2 feet height filled with water. The water tank had two external extensions, one long and the other concise, to easily accommodate different weapons according to the length of their barrels. The examiner at the gun unit took Lawrence's loaded handgun to the water tank and shot a bullet through the tank. He opened the tank's cover and used a long tweezer to pluck the bullet from the bottom of the water tank. Then he took it to a screen for side-by-side comparison under the wondering eyes of the two agents, who couldn't wait for the outcome. The comparison was projected on a big screen where everyone in the unit could see the perfect match of the bullet fired into the tank and the bullets from the crime scenes. The barrel of Lawrence's handgun left some unique microscopic marks on the bullets identical to all three bullets recovered. Agent Frank demanded that the same test be done to all the bullets loaded in Lawrence's handgun to ensure a hundred per cent accuracy. The examiner examined all the bullets from Lawrence's office, but they all told the same story. It took the two FBI agents the whole day of testing to determine that Mr. Lawrence Jackson was the sole perpetrator of the murder of Michelle Cornett and Mrs. Menefee. Agents Frank and Bryan were thrilled to realize their endeavor paid off after many hours of sacrifice and dedication. They were happy and gave each other a high-five, then hopped on a plane the next day to Atlanta. After they secured an arrest warrant around 10:30 a.m., the two agents went to the Lawrence Jackson Insurance Agency, and Brenda Morales recognized them and opened the door for them. They asked about her boss, and the young lady pointed to the back office where the two agents found Lawrence Jackson. They placed him under arrest for the murder of Michelle Cornett and Katie Menefee by citing the famous quotation:" You are under arrest for the murder of Michelle Cornett and Katie Menefee. You have the right to remain silent, and anything you say can be used against you in court. You have the right to an attorney. If you cannot afford an attorney, one will be provided. Do you understand the rights I have just read to you? Do you wish to speak to me with these rights?". He shook his head, stretched his hands to the back to be handicapped, and followed the agents without hesitation or resisting the arrest. Lawrence was taken to the Fulton County Jail on Rice Street in Atlanta for the booking process and was given chance to call his wife. He instructed his wife to find a good attorney for him as soon as possible because his case was severe. He still had $32,000 in his bank account to secure an experienced criminal attorney. His wife, Bernice, was befuddled and didn't believe it possible that her husband would have been involved in a crime in any shape or form. Lawrence was fingerprinted and photographed, was given new inmate outfits, and was ushered to the criminal wing of the prison. He was thrown into a cell occupied by two other criminals who weren't happy to have an additional inmate in their cell. After the booking process, special agent Frank took the evidence against Lawrence to the Fulton County District Attorney France Williams' office in Atlanta. Agent Frank and District Attorney Frances had worked on a previous case involving a young lady who was a beneficiary of many US army soldiers' life policies. Agent Frank warned the DA not to release Lawrence on bail because he was bringing a hitman in town to carry out a murder on his behalf. The two longtime friends reviewed evidence and agreed on the procedure to convict the insurance agent without any ambiguity. They listened to some recordings between Lawrence and his wife to determine whether his wife was aware of his scheme or not. He left the DA office happy to close this chapter of his carrier and was waiting for another one to open soon. Bernice was heartbroken and didn't know whom to turn to. She cried when she called her mother, who advised her to go to the Cochran Law Firm in Atlanta to retain a criminal attorney. After leaving her children with a babysitter, she entered the Cochran firm to find an experienced lawyer to bring her husband home. Bernice was assigned a long-time crime advocate, lawyer Paul Frazier, who immediately called the DA's office to know the charges against his client. After inquiring about the case, attorney Paul Frazier assured Bernice of a successful outcome of the case and charged $15,000. Bernice wrote an initial check of $10,000 to attorney Frazier to start working on the case as soon as possible. Attorney Frazier rushed to the Fulton County Jail to meet with Lawrence Jackson for the initial concertation. The meeting between attorney Frazier and Lawrence took about twenty minutes, and the two men couldn't agree on a strategy to get a successful result. For the lawyer, if no eyewitness could identify Lawrence as the murderer, attorney Frazier was confident to inject a little uncertainty into the jury's decision. Lawrence was under a tremendous guilt and would like to take responsibility for the death of the two women because of his greed. The two men met the following day after Lawrence's first court appearance to meet his judge wishing to be released on bond. Lawrence was instructed not to say anything about his guilt, for the attorney Frazier would be at his side for his first court proceedings. The following week, early in the morning, he embarked with seven other inmates in the Fulton County jail white van to meet judge David Wallace who presided over his case. The van took them to the Fulton County Superior Court on Roswell Road in Atlanta, where Lawrence met with judge Wallace for the first time. Lawrence didn't say a word, but his lawyer spoke on his behalf, not trying to enter any plea deal yet. He just nodded when the judge wanted to ensure he understood all the charges against him. The judge reread the charges and explained that Lawrence would serve a sixty-year prison term in a federal penitential if found guilty. Attorney Frazier briefly chatted with the judge, who gave him some paperwork containing the different charges against his client and gave them a week to return to court. Lawrence was escorted back to a waiting room by a sheriff to wait on the rest of his crew so they could get on the white county jail van to the prison. Before he left the presence of Judge Wallace, attorney Frazier reassured him that he would come to see him in the jail to have a serious conversation on the case. On the way back to the jail, Lawrence felt like a bird in a cage, seeing the sunshine and people on the street enjoying their freedom. The city was looking different in his eyes. The roads were immaculate, the people walking sideways were so beautiful, and the building in the far distance was so pretty. He had never seen this side of the city of Atlanta before that compelled his admiration and contemplation. He wished the ride would last a little longer, but they were at the double gate of the prison at no time. Before the shackle and the handcuff were taken off, Lawrence was informed that he had visitors waiting for him since the morning. It was his wife, and the two kids would like to meet him and hear why he couldn't come home to see his family. His heart started racing fast while a hot sweat trickled down his face, and he didn't know how to explain the situation to his wife. With sadness on the face, he didn't even know where or how to start the conversation with his wife and the two children. Lawrence was led into a large hall with many telephone booths with assigned numbers. He was told to enter booth number five, where his visitors were waiting on the other side of the hall. He went into booth five, where he could see his wife and the two children through a tick glass window that separated them. His heart broke instantly, and he wanted to embrace his wife and the two kids, but he couldn't. He was bleeding inside when he picked up the phone to hear his wife's voice, whose face still showed signs of tears being wiped away. He admitted everything to Bernice and told her his trial might take longer; in which case she should move to her parents in Cobb County. He even instructed his wife to close his insurance business and turned the keys of the facility to the property's landlord. Then Lawrence asked his wife to put his son Joshua on the phone so that he could talk to him after these few days of a brutal separation. He assured his son that he would be coming home soon and that he loved him so much. Lawrence asked his son to put his younger sister Grace on the phone, so he could also speak to her and assure her of his love for her. He was on the phone with Grace hearing her little pleading voice asking him to come home because she missed him so much. Bernice cried when she heard her daughter pleading with her daddy to come home because she wasn't sleeping without him. She didn't know how to tell her that her daddy was in a big trouble and that he wouldn't be coming home anytime soon.

"Hi, Grace; how are you doing?"

"Not so good. I miss you".

"I miss you too."

"Why can you come home to see us?"

"Yeah, I'll come sometime."

"Can you come home today so I can sleep well?"

"It can't be today."

"Why? But you have said you love me and wanted to be with us".

"I know, but things happen."

"So, you love people here more than us?"

"No, it's not like that."

"So, come home so I can have a good sleep."

"I assure you that ......" Then the correctional officer came in to cut short the conversation. The twenty-minute-visitation was over.

Lawrence didn't like how the visit ended, but he didn't have the power to object to any ill-treatment he had been going through since the first day he was incarcerated. He was heartbroken to see his wife and children walk away, and a handcuff was put on his two hands and ushered back to his solitary confinement. He cried so much the rest of the day and couldn't eat any food offered because the shock of the separation from his family was unbearable.

In the evening, the attorney Frazier talked sternly with Lawrence about the strategy in court proceedings. Attorney Frazier reviewed different methods to get him out of trouble because there was no DNA on the crime scenes and no eyewitnesses to link him to the murders. It was a case of a lack of substantial evidence linking Lawrence to the two crime scenes, attorney Frazier would convince the jury to side with him. Even after reviewing the success rate of his carrier as a criminal attorney, attorney Frazier could not persuade Lawrence, who was still maintaining his guilty plea bargain. Frustrated, attorney Frazier called District Attorney France Williams' office to indicate his decision for a guilty plea. The DA reassured him that she would pass the information to her assistant and the judge for the next court date. When the next court date came around, attorney Frazier and assistant district attorney John Welsh met in the hallway for a quick deal striking. When Lawrence was brought to the courtroom, he sat beside attorney Frazier looking at the assistant DA on the far left. Judge David Wallace entered the courtroom in a long black garment in less than ten minutes. In a loud voice, the court clerk announced his presence: "All rise. Court is now in session; the Honorable Judge David Wallace is presiding". He took Lawrence's folder to the judge's desk and handed it to the judge. Then Honorable Judge David Wallace presided over Lawrence's case as follows:

"In the matter of the State vs. Lawrence Jackson. Mr. Jackson, how do you plead?"

"Guilty," Lawrence said.

"Counsel, have you reached a settlement deal?" the judge said.

"Yes, your Honor. We have agreed to a prison time served and payment to the close parents affected by the crimes," John Welsh answered.

"Mr. Lawrence, do you know that by pleading guilty, you lose the right to a jury trial?" the judge said.

"Yes, your Honor," Lawrence said.

"Do you give up that right?" the judge emphasized.

"Yes, your Honor," Lawrence replied.

"Do you understand what giving up that right means?" the judge asked.

"Yes," Lawrence said.

"Do you know that you are waiving the right to cross-examine your accusers?" the judge said.

"Yes, your Honor," Lawrence added.

"Do you know you are waiving your privilege against self-incrimination?" the judge continued.

"Yes," Lawrence said.

"Did anyone force you into accepting this settlement?" the judge insisted.

"No, your Honor," Lawrence answered.

"Are you pleading guilty because you killed the two victims?" the judge continued.

"Yes," Lawrence admitted.

"Mr. Jackson, I have scheduled your sentencing day in two months" the judge closed the session and sent a copy of the session to attorney Paul Frazier and the assistant DA. A court Sheriff came and grabbed Lawrence by the hands to put a handcuff on them and took him back to the waiting room. Attorney Frazier and the assistant D.A. returned to the hallway for quick concertation before the two men went their separate ways. Lawrence was taken into the County Jail van with other inmates returning to the jail where he shared a cell with two vicious criminals. It was a bright shining day, and many people were about their daily activities outside. He saw a man walking on the sideway with his son holding his hand and reverently talking to each other. Lawrence was biting his lips as he admired the incredible scenery of people going and coming throughout Atlanta. The sun was almost in the middle of the sky sending bright golden rays on Downtown Atlanta skyscrapers. The beauty of the city from distance was stunning and some birds who were flying over the city made it looked like a fairy town. As always, the ride to the prison gates was too short.

Chapter 11

Lawrence Jackson sentencing date

The probation officer, Jacob Zulu, assigned to Lawrence's case, went to work diligently to facilitate the completion of comprehensive assessments of the case. He gathered all public records about Lawrence Jackson from birth to adulthood and information about his relatives. He contacted Lawrence's older brother Mike on the upcoming sentencing date. Mike was living in Lithonia, Georgia, where he was an assistant manager of a marine battery company that paid him well. He bought a house for his wife and children and had his sick mother in his basement. Mike was shocked to learn that his brother was in serious trouble with the laws and was on the way to a federal prison. The probation officer contacted Laura in California, who was in the hospital delivering her third child and didn't sympathize with her younger brother. Then the probation office moved to the victims' close family members, who were deeply affected by the loss of the two women involved in Lawrence Jackson's case. John Welch visited Mr. Gerald Menefee to learn what he was going through after losing his lovely wife. The men had a long conversation to assess the day-to-day challenges Mr. Gerald Menefee was facing, and Mr. Jacob Zulu instructed him on what to bring to the court on the sentencing date. Gerald had difficulty paying the rent of the apartment he was sharing with his wife since her income stopped coming in. Moreover, he couldn't pay on the car note of the 2024 Tesla X300 because he didn't know how to budget his finance, which was his wife's prerogative. Mr. Jacob Zulu reached out to Brendon Lyle, Michelle Cornett's son living with his father, Henry Lyle, in New Jersey. The boy was going through severe hardship since he moved in with his father and didn't know if he could finish high school successfully. He couldn't get along with his stepmother, who considered him a threat to the well-being of her two daughters fathered by Henry Lyle. She threw him out of the house couple of times, and his academic performance was deficient. Mr. Jacob Zulu urged him to send a letter of hardship to the court for the upcoming murder trial of his mother on September 5th. In preparation for the sentencing day, attorney Paul Frazier called Bernice Jackson to inform her about the plea bargain for less punishment time her husband decided on would be held on September 5th. During the discussion, attorney Paul Frazier realized Bernice was too emotional to stand between the judge and her husband to ask for any favor. Finally, she wrote a letter to the judge to ask for a lesser punishment since her husband has zero official criminal histories. She knew he was a good man and didn't know what went through his mind to commit a murder.

On the sentencing day, the courtroom was parked by 8:30 a.m., and many deputies' sheriffs were brought in to ease tensions between the parties. When Judge David Wallace came in, he ordered the audience to be quiet before proceeding. The victims' family members were verbally threating Bernice.

They believed Bernice was a complicit with her husband in the murder of their loved ones. After the judge ensured everyone in the courtroom was silent, he ordered the sheriffs to bring the defendant in. Lawrence was in a grey Fulton County Jail outfit and was ordered to sit next to his lawyer. He knew the courtroom was full of people but couldn't tell who was in the crowd. The Dove family, Michelle Cornett's co-workers, Camp Creek Middle School teachers, staff, Fulton County Public Schools District representatives, US Army Colonels, and more were in the courtroom. Liz and Andrew Dove were ashamed of Lawrence's misconduct and came to the trial to support their daughter and her children. Judge David Wallace opened a blue file on his desk and started.

"In the matter of the State of Georgia VS Lawrence Jackson, Case# 78105," stated the judge in a deep baritone voice that echoed throughout the courtroom.

"Counsels, do you plan to appeal the court's judgment?" the judge asked.

"Your Honor, we don't plan to appeal your decision," answered attorney Paul Frazier.

"Does the defendant understand waiving his right to a jury trial?" the judge turned his attention to Lawrence to ensure he was aware of his right.

"Yes, your honor," replied Lawrence Jackson.

"Can the prosecution team call the first witness to stand?" added the judge.

"Mr. Gerald Menefee to the stand," voiced the assistant DA.

"State your name and relationship with the victim," the judge instructed Mr. Gerald.

"My name is Mr. Gerald Menefee, and I'm the husband of the late Katie Menefee," Mr. Gerald told the court.

"Take a seat and proceed," ordered the judge.

Mr. Gerald Menefee had a four-page note containing all he was going through physically, mentally, emotionally, and financially since the tragic separation with his wife. He started painting Lawrence as a soulless, cruel individual with no feelings and greedy beyond measure. Each time he mentioned any negative qualification of Lawrence, Bernice would whisper to herself, "It's not true." Mr. Gerald couldn't finish reading his four page-note because his emotion took over his body, and many in the audience were crying too. Lawrence Jackson couldn't hold his tear for the first time; the magnitude of his senseless actions overcame the toughness of his heart. When Brendon Lyle took the stand, Lawrence Jackson couldn't raise his head to see the boy in the face. Instead, the boy was very prepared and vividly compared his mother to his stepmother, who made his life miserable. The judge cut him short to get to the sentencing and the final phase of the court hearing. Judge David Wallace sentenced Lawrence to thirty years on count one and three years on count two, which was reduced because of Lawrence's plea deal. He was sentenced to a thirty-three-year maximum security term in a federal prison in North Carolina and would pay a fine of $20,000 for restitution. Two deputy sheriffs ushered Lawrence out of the courtroom shortly after the sentencing. His wife Bernice burst into tears seeing her husband in shackles who could hardly walk. Liz and Andrew tried in vain to comfort her in the courtroom; even the intervention of the attorney Paul Frazier couldn't help. Outside the courtroom, gathered the victims' close family members who weren't satisfied with judge David Wallace's sentence. Some of them found the sentence not strict enough and argued to form a team and send a letter to the judge to sentence Lawrence to a sixty-year prison term without parole. Others found sending a letter to the judge unnecessary because the latter considered the defense team's plea bargain deal. Without that, it should have been a lengthy trial. The victims' family members had different degrees of satisfaction with the verdict. Lawrence was taken into the Fulton County Jail white van with other inmates who also appeared in court for their respective cases. The white van was at the jail's double gates when Lawrence realized he didn't have a chance to admire the festive activities of people on the roads leading from the courthouse to the prison. He couldn't take the sentencing lightly because he didn't think he could survive a thirty-three-year prison term. Liz and Andrew took Bernice to her apartment in College Park and booked a U-HAUL truck to collect all the Jacksons' belongings. Andrew hired two laborers at the Home Depot nearby to help load the heavy items in the apartment. After emptying the apartment, the two laborers drove with Andrew to Cobb County, where they discharged the U-HAUL in the Dove's house. Bernice grabbed her two children from the babysitter and moved in with her parents in Cobb County. Before leaving College Park for good, Bernice returned to the leasing office of the apartment complex the house keys and the mailbox keys. The leasing manager inquired about Lawrence, but Bernice couldn't give her an account of how the trial went. By the end of the day, the attorney Paul Frazier called Bernice to return some of the money she paid to save Lawrence from going to prison. The attorney was so upset about Lawrence, who wouldn't take the chance to go through a jury trial where he could possibly avoid incarceration.

The next day Lawrence was put, around 4:00 p.m., in the County Jail van in chains in the company of two jail guards to the Onslow federal prison in North Carolina. The prison was isolated in a deserted area surrounded by bushes and tall oak trees with no habitation anywhere close. They got to the new location around 9:00 p.m., and all the prisoners were in their respective ceil with lights on. Lawrence didn't know why he was being transferred to federal prison in Onslow County on a peach dark night. The federal prison was located on a vast land in the middle of nowhere, surrounded by two twelve feet tall wire fences. A six-foot distance between the two fences made the structure looked like a corridor around the prison. At the four corners of the fences were four towers where security guards permanently monitored the inmates and any suspicious activity inside or outside the detention facility. There was a single door to the prison for the employees and visitors. It was guarded by two police Officers who controlled the identities and the motives of visitations. They determined who could come into the prison and who shouldn't come by checking the criminal records of all visitors. On the other side were two large gates controlled by heavily armed security guards. One large gate was in the first fence, and the second large gate was embedded in the second fence. The two large gates didn't open simultaneously to allow inspection of any vehicle entering the prison yard. The first large gate must be closed before the guards could open the second one. Between the two fences, right next to the second large gate, was a brown all-in glass booth where people could see all the electronic equipment guards used to get information on individuals and vendors accessing the prison facilities. In front of the single door, from the outside, was a big parking lot where the employees and the visitors could park their cars. A sign on the fence showed the visitation time to be between 9:00 a.m. and 12:00 p.m. for all inmates, no exceptions. In the center of the vast land surrounded by the two wire fences were the two inmate facilities, which were in a significant bloc in a rectangular shape. On the right side of the building was the first housing facility, which consisted of three hundred prison cells occupied by two inmates each. The second housing facility was on the left side of first the block, duplicating exactly the first housing facility. All the prison cells had an opening of thirty inches by fifteen inches covered with a solid glass, allowing the inmates to glance at the weather outside. The two housing facilities were three-story-building about six hundred meters long linked to each other at each end. Between the two housing facilities was a significant playground with two young trees, where the inmates could play basketball games or just come out to enjoy the bright sun. The only access to the playground was through the large lunchroom at the bottom of each housing block. The prison was built and operated to give the inmates the almost impossible chance to escape, whether in broad daylight or at night. Lawrence got stripped of his Fulton County Jail outfit, put on a multiple strips uniform, and led to his new cell on the third floor of the first housing facility. He was sharing a cell with Jason Sullivan, who had already completed seven years of his ten-year prison term. Lawrence was replacing Jason's former roommate, who exhausted his prison sentence and was released a week ago. Contrary to his experience, the two inmates bounded and talked about their life story all night. The two inmates had a lot in common. They both had childhood trauma and were married struggling to make ends meet.

Jason Sullivan was a security guard in a federal-insured Bank of America in Los Angeles, California. Jason started working for the bank right after his high school diploma and rented an apartment on South Hoover Street to get closer to his job, which was about three miles away. He married his high school sweetheart, who was living with him but was having trouble giving birth because of multiple miscarriages she had experienced. The couple consulted many physicians who couldn't help but offered them the comfort to keep trying, and it wasn't too late. This situation dragged the couple into financial difficulties that made it impossible to meet ends. Jason decided to ride his bike to work less than three miles from his apartment to minimize expenses. He had been working in the bank for over five years and knew all the bank's routines and the management rotations. Between his apartment and his job was a vacant lot that Jason passed by every day, going to or returning from work. The vacant lot was located at the corner of Hoover Street and W. Vernon Avenue. Jason never knew whom the lot belonged to, but he used to play there with children in the neighborhood when he was young. The land always had some dry grasses and a couple of trees by the cement fence with two openings and an abandoned house without a roof.

Jason was a diligent employee who earned his income honestly, but one day he argued with himself about the way he was earning his living. He was convinced that there should be a better way. One Friday morning of a fourth of July long weekend, Jason went to work by 8:00 a.m. and opened the bank as soon as the senior manager turned off the establishment's alarms. By 8:15 a.m., the Armor Truck dropped in a black leather bag containing $400,000 for the Bank ATM transaction over the long weekend. While the manager was busy setting up the bank for business, Jason turned off the backdoor alarms and the surveillance cameras in the facility. The assistant manager, Kendra, would come to work before 8:30 a.m. Jason reached out to take the back leather bag with the ATM money and went through the backdoor, where he parked his bike. He rode the bike to the vacant lot where he dug a hole along the cement fence the previous night and covered it with a large plastic. He quickly dropped the ATM money in the hole, covered it with dirt and dry grass, and continued his way home. When the assistant manager Kendra came to work, Jason was nowhere to be found, and the ATM money had disappeared. The manager wanted to check the surveillance cameras to see what was happening but realized that the backdoor alarm and cameras were caught off. They called the police on Jason, who was at home when two police officers arrived. He denied any involvement with the ATM money's disappearance, claimed he wasn't feeling good at work and came home to sleep. The police searched and ransacked his apartment but could find the money. The bank pressed charges against Jason and sentenced him to ten years in prison. He was incarcerated in different federal prisons until he was transferred to the Onslow Federal Jail in North Carolina. After three years of incarceration, his wife divorced him and married a school janitor who gave her three children.

Chapter 12

Lawrence Jackson's prison time

Jason Sullivan reviewed the "dos and don'ts" in the Onslow federal prison which all inmates should abide by to survive. Lawrence understood that he shouldn't discuss his case with any other inmate, for anything he said could be used against him in court; even his family members could end up as a witness against him. The prison personnel reviewed all letters, and phone calls in and out of the prison to find any suspicious elements in inmates' cases. The Onslow Jail was divided into a couple of blocks, Block A and Block B, with an equally same number of inmates. All the inmates were confined to their cells for twenty-two hours a day and utilized the two remaining hours for personal, such as shower time, lunch time and playground time. Every day, Block A would go to lunch at noon for thirty minutes and proceed to the playground for another half-hour before returning to the cells. At 12:30 p.m.,. Block B would go to lunch while Block A was heading to the playground, which Block B would occupy after Block A left. Inmates could use their playground time for gym workouts or a shower. If a fight broke out in a Block, all the Block inmates would go into lockdown, losing their leisure time and returning to their respective cells. The inmates involved in the fight would go to solitary confinement for a week, where they couldn't eat with others or enjoy playtime. Some correctional officers or good inmates would bring their food to their confinement cell, and all reading materials would be taken away from them except the bible. They could get a monitored time for showers and phone calls followed by correctional officers. Using drug in Onslow Jail was strongly prohibited, and any inmate caught using the illegal drug would go to solitary confinement for a month. The jail administration conducted random drug tests on all inmates, and anyone testing positive would cause tension. The jail authorities would check all the surveillance cameras to find the origin of the drug on the jail property. Any visitor smuggling an illegal drug into the prison would be prosecuted, sentenced to a five-year prison term, and paid a heavy fine. In the Onslow jail, the inmates had to get in line when to consult a psychiatrist, a nurse, or an investigator. Services in the prison were offered on a first-come and first-serve basis, and inmates weren't allowed to cut in front of other inmates. Cutting in front of other inmates in Onslow prison was treating other inmates as punk, which inevitably would lead to fights. Every fight would lead to a lockdown and confinement for those involved in the conflict. Finally, the Onslow federal prison offered other activities to the inmates to get active and earn money and education. Inmates with good social behavior could apply for additional workout times in the fully equipped prison gym. Some with good behavior records could apply to work in the sowing facility to earn extra money in the prison. They could work seven hours a day and earn up to two hundred dollars monthly to care for basic needs in prison. Others could apply to take college courses in the jail to graduate with a bachelor's degree in English, Science, and General Study. Every educational institute across the United States of America accepted a degree from the Onslow Federal Prison.

Two months after being transferred to the Onslow Federal Jail, Lawrence Jackson received a visit from his wife with some troubling questions.

"How is your life in prison?" asked Bernice.

"It's not easy, but I'm taking it one day at a time," answered Lawrence.

"Thirty-three years is a long time," affirmed Bernice.

"Yeah, it's a long time," confirmed Lawrence.

"Being in my shoes, can you wait for me for thirty-three years?" asked Bernice.

"Well, well," Lawrence couldn't answer the question.

"I don't have that strength to carry on for thirty-three years," Bernice ended the conversation.

She drove back to Cobb County crying, knowing that her marriage couldn't survive this tragic separation. After the first visit, Liz Dove introduced her daughter to different fine men from her church, expecting to find a better husband for Bernice, who showed considerable sign of depression. Liz and Andrew Dove occasionally organized a barbeque cookout in their garden, decorated with exotic flowers, for the church single-men group to help Bernice meet other men. Still, Bernice was so much in her cocoon and wouldn't take the bait. Instead, she concentrated more on her two children's education and didn't take a good care of herself. Lawrence also stopped calling her from the jail because Liz always complained that the jail collect-calls ran high her monthly phone bill. She negatively interjected Lawrence and his two children or cut their conversations short. Bernice didn't like how her mother mistreated her husband, who was incarcerated and needed support from the outside.

After a year of proven good behavior in Onslow Federal Jail, Lawrence enrolled in college credits courses for a science degree. He didn't know why he chose the Science Degree path, but he knew thirty-three years was a considerable amount of time to accomplish anything. He couldn't go to college because he had no support after the tragic death of his father, and his mother couldn't provide sufficiently for the family. In that condition, he chose the insurance school and started working after his high school diploma. This was a golden opportunity for him to get a degree in jail, even if it would take thirty-three years to be completed. Lawrence also secured two days' work in the sowing facility, where he could make $70 a month. An income of $70 in jail was a considerable amount of money to purchase snacks and candy bars, which were rare commodities in Onslow Federal Jail. Lawrence was so glad to get involved with school and a little job which kept him busy in jail and helped him avoid the jailhouse dramas going around him daily. The North Carolina Department of Safety administered the degree programs, which hired college professors to deliver college courses in the prison. The department utilized the Governor's Crime Commission Grants to pay for the lessons and the materials for the inmates to get a good education. The US Department of Education indicated that criminal offenders who participated in educational activities while incarcerated had a better chance to become responsible and productive citizens who could effectively make outstanding contributions to their community. Jason Sullivan wouldn't get involved in schooling because he argued he wanted to go into business for himself upon release. His mind was set up on a modern laundromat in South Central Los Angeles, where a sizeable low-income population lived in California. He had chosen the name "The Spin Town Laundromat" for the laundromat he would manage himself. When the first one would become successful, he would open another in a different area of Los Angeles. Jason had a great business plan to convince his wife, who gave him a divorce letter, in prison. He didn't want to discuss where he would get the capital to start up the presumed laundromat business. He wanted to write her about where the money would come from. Still, he knew the prison authorities meticulously reviewed all letters and phone calls. He took extreme precautions not to reveal where the money would come from to purchase his business's commercial wash machines and dryers. He was the only one who knew the hideout of the bank ATM money, for which he was serving time in jail.

Lawrence Jackson was so involved in his schooling that he couldn't tell how fast the time was running. It was hard for him to say goodbye to his roommate Jason Sullivan the day he purged his sentence and was released from prison. The two men hugged each other for a long time and didn't want to end their friendship. Jason earned enough money in jail to buy a greyhound bus ticket from North Carolina to Los Angeles,

California. Jason promised to write Lawrence when he got to Los Angeles and started his business in South Central. A promise Jason Sullivan had never kept because of the surprises that were awaiting him in the City of Los Angeles.

When his roommate left, Lawrence was having trouble with the advanced Chemistry 202 and was requesting tutorial assistance from the prison administration. He loved chemistry so much that he wouldn't quit, but he needed help with additional materials to grasp the concept he was being taught. Besides his struggle to make it through the college courses and get a degree, his wife and father-in-law came to serve him with divorce papers. He signed the documents with a broken heart but knew his marriage wouldn't survive a thirty-three-year incarceration test. What Lawrence didn't know was that Liz finally found a new husband for her daughter, who was at the point of getting married. He couldn't blame her, but himself. But, he hated the fact that another man would raise his two children in his absence.

Chapter 13

Lawrence Jackson was devoted to studying science

Lawrence scheduled an appointment to meet with the high prison chief, Andy Campbell, to express his concerns about the learning he was getting in the prison. The high prison chief relayed Lawrence's legitimate requests to the North Carolina Department of Safety, explaining how the inmate's conditions weren't conducive to learning. In three weeks of discussion, the Governor's Crime Commission Grants offered a new desk to Lawrence. He received many books about his study courses and a personal tutor who graduated from the University of North Carolina in Science. The private tutor, Bob Scott, visited Lawrence in prison every Saturday to cover everything that might trouble him in his study ranging from English to Math. Bob Scott would recommend additional study materials, which the Governor's Crime Commission Grants would pay. Lawrence was doing well and keeping up with his homework, numerous assignments, and projects. Most of the classes were long-distance courses, and his instructions noticed his fantastic effort to complete all work on time and accurately.

One night, Lawrence had a dream. In the dream, he saw his science teacher standing next to a six-foot-tall tree in a large field. The science teacher pointed to the tree's body:

"This is a living creature. It has a front and a back. It stores the picture of every moving object or person that passes within a six-foot radius".
"How to get the image?" asked Lawrence.

"Cut the cork of the front of the tree if you need an image from the front," said the teacher.

"Why is that?" questioned Lawrence.

"Images in the back are different from the one in the front of the tree," he answered.

"How to extract the picture?" asked Lawrence.

"Have a clean container containing magnesium chloride (MgCl2, H2O). Put a whole cork in the solution and add vinegar to submerge the cork," replied the teacher.

"What kind of vinegar is required?" asked Lawrence.

"Red vinegar yields colorful pictures whether it occurs at night or daytime," answered the teacher.

"Does the climate affect the pictures?" asked Lawrence.

"Keep the cork in the solution for twenty-four hours in a dark room before attempting to collect the images," replied the science teacher.

Lawrence woke out of his sleep, remembering every detail of the conversation in his dream. He reached out to his watch on his study desk to realize that it was 3:45 a. m. and couldn't go back to sleep. His mind was wrestling with the dream, trying to process it and find a meaning to all of this. The thought came to his mind to talk to his science teacher the next day or wait until the following Saturday to go over it with his tutor. He highly regarded his science teacher and Mr. Bob Scott, who had a tremendous amount of knowledge in science. The prison was very quiet. He was alone in his cell and had no one to talk to. He went to his study desk to continue with some homework he was working on the previous night before sleep got on him. He mastered Trigonometric exercises due to his tutor's help, who constantly infused the spirit of "Yes, I can." Lawrence went back to sleep around 6:30 a. m. to get up by noon to line up for lunch in the prison breakroom. At lunch, the idea came to him to share his dream with other inmates sitting at his lunch table, but he rejected that feeling because he couldn't trust anyone in the prison. A little misunderstanding could become a bloody fight, and the weaker in the conflict would wind up in the hospital for days or weeks.

There was zero tolerance among the inmates who could be friends today and adversaries the following day over a meaningless argument. Lawrence fought hard to keep himself out of trouble and didn't want to take any chance of jeopardizing his degree in science at the end of his incarceration. A fight could break next to him at any time between two inmates where one believed he was disrespected by the other by cutting in front of him during a lineup or calling him a "Punk." Not long ago, an inmate beat the "crap" out of another inmate by using padlocks inside socks and hitting the other inmate on the head. The injured inmate's brain was swollen, and he was taken to the hospital and never returned to the prison. Nobody knew what the outcome of the injury the inmate sustained was. Nobody knew if he survived the beating of his head with padlocks in a sock or if he died in the hospital. The correctional officers couldn't always protect all inmates. Instead, they tried their best to anticipate conflicts before they turned into bloody fights, but the inmates outnumbered them so much that they got surprised from time to time.

After the daily recreational activity, Lawrence and the other inmates were ushered back to the prison housing area. Lawrence returned to his cell and to his study desk to finish the trigonometric homework he was working on earlier. As usual, he forgot all the thoughts troubling him during the day and went to bed around 10:30 p.m. with unusual fatigue. Lawrence had the same dream he had the previous night. It was an identical dream where he interacted with his science teacher, pointing at a young six-foot-tall tree in a field:

"This is a living organism. It has a front and a back. It stores the picture of every moving object or person that passes within a six-foot radius".

"How to get the image?" asked Lawrence.

"Cut the cork of the front of the tree if you need an image from the front," said the teacher.

"Why is that?" questioned Lawrence.

"Images in the back are different from the one in the front of the tree," he answered.

"How to extract the picture?" asked Lawrence.

"Have a clean container containing magnesium chloride ($MgCl_2$, H_2O). Put a whole cork in the solution and add vinegar to submerge the cork," replied the teacher.

"What kind of vinegar is required?" asked Lawrence.

"Red vinegar yields colorful pictures whether it occurs at night or daytime," answered the teacher.

"Does the climate affect the pictures?" asked Lawrence.

"Keep the cork in the solution for twenty-four hours in a dark room before attempting to collect the images," replied the science teacher.

Lawrence woke up. He was widely awake and realized he had the same dream with his science teacher pointing to a tree in a field. He went slowly to his study desk to verify the time and was baffled that it was 3:45 a.m. on his watch. He acknowledged that this wasn't a coincidence and that the dream elements had a significant meaning. The thought came through his mind to write down vividly every dream detail in a special notebook that he could keep secret. Lawrence put the notebook under his pillow after writing down the dream and decided to talk to his science teacher about the virtue of a tree cork. He was sure his science teacher had more information about tree corks that he might want to give away. He sent a message to his science teacher about a severe matter he wanted to discuss over the phone. Two days later, the teacher called the prison to discuss a concern with Lawrence Jackson, one of his faithful prison students. The two men had a fifteen-minute-long dialogue. Lawrence was very disappointed in his science teacher, who gave him a long lecture about the essence of dreams and why scientists had never considered them. He was upset that his science teacher didn't give him a chance to explain the dream's content before his harsh judgment.

Lawrence was so convinced that the cork theory was significant that he needed to crack it. His other option was Bob Scott, his science tutor, who would meet with him during his tutoring session the following Saturday. When the two science students met, Lawrence was excited to go over his cork theory before any learning could occur. Bob Scott was quiet, listening to Lawrence the whole time he explained the virtue of tree cork to compile images for the long term. After Lawrence finished his lecture on the goodness of tree cork, Bob Scott said:

"Can we get back to learning now?" asked Bob Scott.

"Yes, but all that doesn't mean anything to you?" replied Lawrence.

"No. It's just a dream. A dream comes from what we see on TV, what we read, and what we think," added Bob Scott.

"But some of them have some hidden meaning," affirmed Lawrence.

"Not the one you just have," replied Bob Scott.

"Why is that?" asked Lawrence.

"Because all trees don't have a cork. Some do have, and some don't have. If it's a universal truth, all trees will possess a cork," Bob Scott ended the discussion and reached out to the Chemistry exercise they were supposed to work on that day. The two men were quiet for some time before continuing with math and chemistry exercises Lawrence had to turn in the following week. After Bob Scott left him for the day, Lawrence vowed not to talk to anyone about his dream again. Three weeks after the incident, Lawrence Jackson had another dream which was the ending knowledge he was looking for, which answered his numerous questions. He saw his science teacher in a room resembling a school lab. He entered a dark room inside the lab to retrieve a transparent plastic container with a big piece of a tree cork submerged in magnesium chloride and vinegar solution. He then laid the container on a desk where he had already set up a bloc of printer papers. He folded two diagonal corners of a printing paper, which he laid gently on the surface of the liquid in the transparent container. He took the slightly wet paper to the dark room and put it on a table. He repeated these scenarios several times and finally returned to sit at his desk after carefully closing the dark room in the lab. After some time, the science teacher returned to the darkroom, which he opened carefully and started taking out the dry printing papers. Each paper had a distinctive picture of people and animals passing near the tree which recorded them in the cork. The science teacher stacked the photos in the order in which the printing papers touched the surface of the liquid in the transparent container to determine the chronological order in which the images occurred. The images on the printing papers were from large to small according to the time the animal or the person got close to the tree. Lawrence said, "This must be a great tool in investigating crimes." Then he woke up. He was widely awakened, reached out to his notebook under his pillow, and walked to his study desk. He wrote every little detail of the science teacher's movements in the dream to add to what he had written in the notebook three weeks ago. After writing down all the elements of his vision, the theory of tree cork became crystal clear in his mind. He was thrilled and looking for someone to hug; he was alone in his cell and started singing a joyful melody of his childhood in College Park. He went to his study desk to check the time and realized that it was only 3:30 in the morning, and it was quiet all around him. An unspeakable joy invaded his entire being, but he didn't know whom to share this revolutionary theory with. The image of his ex-wife and his two children came to his mind. He wished they were there to share this incredible moment that could be a game-changer in his life.

Meanwhile, Bernice married Leonardo James, the youth Pasteur in her parents' congregation in Cobb County. The marriage celebration was held in the Dove family garden at the back of their house. Leonardo was a humble and God-fearing servant with no significant life ambitions. That resonated loudly with Bernice, who wanted to find a simple man she could spend the rest of her life with, far from drama. Leonardo was perfect for her because of his tenderness; he couldn't even harm a fly. He worked with children at the Assembly of God of Cobb County, teaching Sunday and vacation bible classes. The two lovers tied the nod in the Cobb County Assembly of God church; only the church members assisted in the matrimonial ceremony. The reception was held in the garden of Liz and Andrew's backyard. Liz and Andrew Dove covered financially the reception to alleviate the financial burden on the newlyweds. After the wedding, the couple rented one bedroom apartment on Sugar Hill Road near the church. Bernice couldn't bring her two children because the couple wasn't making enough money to take care of the kids. Joshua and Grace were left to the care of Liz and Andrew, who would do anything for Bernice to have a happy home. Leonardo perceived a monthly income from the church, but his salary was just enough for him and his wife. Any extra burden would destabilize the new home and cause Bernice to seek a nine-to-five job. Bernice hadn't held a steady employment for the past five years and lived off her husband and two parents, who loved her dearly. She focused more on the education of her two children, who showed signs of imbalance since they were separated from their loving and caring father. Joshua was becoming more and more aggressive in school, while Grace was becoming more and more introverted. She lost all interest in classroom activities, which affected her academic performance.

Chapter 14

Lawrence Jackson, in the line of detectives.

For six months, Lawrence Jackson was maturing his cork theory in his mind and wouldn't let it out of his mouth to any inmates. Every night for the last six months, Lawrence revisited his notebook under his pillow, first to ensure it wasn't tempered and second to know it was still there.

One morning, Lawrence gathered all his strength to see the high prison chief Andy Campbell in his office to expose his cork theory as a diligent science major student. Mr. Andy Campbell received Lawrence in his office and allowed him to reveal the benefits of his tree cork theory in detail. After exposing the basis of his theory, Lawrence took time and efficiently answered all the high prison chief's questions. Lawrence offered two hundred dollars to Mr. Andy Campbell at the end of their conversation to purchase the elements he needed to test his claim. Lawrence gave the money he earned by working in the sowing facility to the high prison chief to buy a plastic container, chloric acid, a powder of magnesium, and a dash of red vinegar. Persuaded by the advantages of the theory, Mr. Andy Campbell collected the money from

Lawrence; he placed an order for all the necessities required to bring the cork theory to life. Then, two weeks later, all elements made it to the high prison chief's office, where Lawrence verified them to meet his satisfaction.

The following day, Andy Campbell took Lawrence to the prison playground and allowed the inmate to cut a piece of cork from one of the two young trees at the edge of the sports area. They both returned to the high prison chief's office, where Lawrence prepared the magnesium chloride by dissolving ten grams of magnesium into a chloric acid. He introduced the cork into the solution and added the red vinegar to submerge the tree cork completely. He put the transparent container with all the elements closed in Andy Campbell's office closet and closed the door with tape to avoid light getting into the closet. Lawrence instructed Andy Campbell not to open the closet door for the next twenty-four hours to allow the tree cork to release all the images in the solution. A correctional officer came in at the request of the high prison chief to escort Lawrence back to his cell over the hostile eyes of the other inmates. Other inmates were suspicious that Lawrence might be talking to the high prison chief about them. They didn't see with good looks that an inmate was talking to the prison administration, no matter the case. Some inmates quickly concluded that Lawrence was leaking a drug deal in preparation for Onslow prison.

The following morning, a correctional officer kindly escorted Lawrence to Mr. Andy Campbell's office, where the chief waited impatiently. The high prison chief instructed the correctional officer to remove the handcuffs from Lawrence's hands and gave them some privacy because the inmate wasn't a threat to him. After the penitentiary officer left, Lawrence retrieved the transparent container from the closet and put it on the office desk. There was already a stack of printing papers on the desk, which Lawrence utilized gently to lay on the surface of the liquid in the transparent container. A total of ten printing papers were used to collect the images and put them in the dark closet to dry for a couple of hours. The high prison chief insisted that Lawrence may stick around his office for three hours, waiting for the printing paper to dry. While waiting for the images, his lunch was brought to Mr. Andy Campbell's office, and a guard collected the tray after he finished. Lawrence was treated with dignity and the respect that he lost from day one he stepped feet in jail in Atlanta, Georgia. Then, around 2 p.m., the two men decided to bring the dry papers out of the dark closet with many expectations in their eyes.

Lawrence removed the tape off the closet door, collected the dry printing papers, and laid them on Andy Campbell's desk in the order in which they were put in the closet. To their big jolt, the printing papers revealed the clear images of many inmates known by the high prison chief and Lawrence. Mr. Andy Campbell was flabbergasted before the collection of the pictures of various inmates and groups of inmates who adverted closer to the tree at the edge of the playground. He marveled by looking Lawrence in the eyes without uttering a word for a long moment with his mouth open. He reached out of his pocket for a brand-new iPhone and called Mr. Charles Daxton, the Chief Detective of the Charlotte-Mecklenburg Police Department.

"Hello, Chief Daxton, how are you doing?" started Andy Campbell.

"Fine, and you, Andy?" replied Mr. Daxton.

"Are you very busy now, Chief Daxton?" asked Mr. Andy Campbell.

"No. What's you got?" answered Mr. Daxton.

"I have a surprise for you in my office," affirmed Mr. Andy Campbell.

"You are in your Onslow Prison office now?" asked Mr. Daxton.

"Can you come and see me?" continued Mr. Andy Campbell

"It depends on the magnitude of the surprise," replied Mr. Daxton.

"This surprise is humongous, and I can't wait to see you here," added Mr. Andy Campbell.

"I'll be there in less than an hour," said Mr. Daxton.

The high prison chief explained to Lawrence who Chief Detective Charles Daxton in North Carolina was. Mr. Charles Daxton was highly regarded in the police and the judiciary system in North Carolina. He was the head of the detective branch of the Charlotte-Mecklenburg Police Department for twenty years and was involved in numerable criminal cases. His success rate was higher than all the previous chief detectives the Charlotte police Department had ever known. He led a team of detectives that highly valued his assessment of crime scenes and convictions procedures. While waiting for the Chief Detective, Mr. Andy Campbell ordered Lawrence a snack from the prison lounge to ensure a friendly atmosphere for the Chief Detective. The Chief Detective was a man of integrity who played fair in all his cases and followed the rules to the letter. He was at the Onslow Prison many times, but the protocols were the same each time, where two correctional officers had to walk him to the high prison chief of the Onslow Prison Office. Mr. Charles Daxton came with his assistant to the prison gates, where he was announced to the high prison chief, who dispatched two correctional officers to walk them to his office. When Mr. Charles Daxton and his assistant entered the high prison chief office, they were stunned to see an inmate in prison uniform sitting by a desk without a handcuff on his hands.

The high prison chief ensured his guests that everything was fine and presented Lawrence Jackson as a brilliant inmate he believed would be excellent access to the police department. The two detectives looked at each other, asking themselves how an inmate could be an excellent access to the police department. Then, Mr. Andy Campbell walked to his desk and showed the detectives the transparent container with the solution and the tree cork inside. Then he handed the inmates and groups of inmates' pictures collected from the liquid in the container. The detectives couldn't wrap their minds around what a drink in a container and photographs of inmates had in common.

Seeing the sign of disconnection on their faces, the high prison chief called upon Lawrence to break down the theory of tree cork for his guests. Lawrence bolding took the stand to explain in detail the origin of the pictures they held. After some questioning, Mr. Andy Campbell testified that all the preparations and the execution of the theory were done before his own eyes. With great amazement, the two detectives promised to return the following day at 10:00 a. m. to take Lawrence to a recent unsolved crime site in Pamlico County. This case involved a dead toddler under a tree wrapped in a dark plastic bag across the street from Pamlico County Wells Fargo Bank on Main Street. The boy was around a year and a half, and the body was found by a morning jogger, who called the police. The police couldn't find any strange DNA trace on the body but used the boy's hair to reconstruct his DNA profile to find his parents. The detectives believed that the person who disposed of the dead body lived in the neighborhood and knew the town well. Bayboro, North Carolina, was a small town where everybody knew everybody, and the population was about three thousand. The police were convinced to solve the case if they could have a picture of the person who jumped the boy under the tree. The tree was a part of a bit of bush along Main Street (NC 55), not far from the Bayboro Wells Fargo Bank, where most residents banked regularly. There was also a significant grocery store, "Food Lion," in the town center where all the residents shopped for food.

Lawrence Jackson spent all day in the high prison chief office before a correctional officer came in and handcuffed him to take him back to his cell. Mr. Andy Campbell wished him a good night until he would see him at 10:00 a.m. when the Chief Detective would be there. While he was led to his cell, other inmates made facial threats and hand gestures toward him. About ten inmates had prepared two socks filled with padlocks to attack him the next time they saw him in the prison lunchroom. These inmates believed Lawrence was snitching on them about their plan to bring in illegal drugs to the high prison chief. Prisoners in the Onslow Jail considered the prison administration an enemy who ambushed them daily to find flaws. Anyone who befriended the administration was also considered an enemy and must be irradicated. When Lawrence finally reached his cell, all the food he had missed for the day was neatly organized on his study desk. He didn't miss any food his friends had for the day. After eating, a correctional officer came to his cell to collect the trays and turned them to the prison lounge. The respect he lost since the first day he was sent to prison gradually returned to him.

The next day at 10:00 a.m. Lawrence was escorted to Mr. Andy Campbell's office, where the Chief Detective and his assistant were waiting for him. When he arrived, the handcuffs were removed from his hands, he got stripped off his jail outfits and was handed new clothes. Lawrence wore brand-new pants and a suit and followed the two detectives to leave the Onslow Prison. They entered a marked police car parked in the parking lot, where Lawrence was presented with photos of the crime scene they were about to visit. He studied the body's position in the black plastic bag very well to figure out precisely what portion of the tree cork he should cut. The three men drove to 715 Main Street, Bayboro, North Carolina, across from the Wells Fargo Bank. Lawrence was given a sharp knife to cut the cork according to the dead body's position at the tree's foot. After cutting the tree cork and safely put in a Ziplock bag, the three men drove to Bayboro's leading grocery store "Food Lion," to purchase a transparent container and red vinegar. Before the three men got into the police-marked car, the Chief Detective ensured Lawrence that he had already purchased the chloric acid and powder magnesium in his office in Charlotte. On their way back, the three men stopped by "Waffle House" for breakfast on behalf of the Chief Detective. When they reached the Chief Detective's office around noon, Lawrence quickly prepared the solution by reacting ten grams of pure magnesium with chloric acid. Then he carefully put the tree cork in the solution and submerged it in red vinegar. He next took the container with the solution and tree cork into a closet in the Chief Detective's office and closed the door tightly. Lawrence advised the Chief not to let anyone open the closet for the next twenty-four hours to allow the full release of images in the solution. The Chief Detective took Lawrence down to the basement of the Charlotte-Mecklenburg Police Department, where hundreds of file cabinets were organized. Chief Charles Daxton showed the file cabinets that contained unsolved murder cases they needed to work on. The two men went through the unsolved murder cases to separate the ones that occurred around a tree or a bush from the others. They dedicated the day to sorting the cold case files for a possible break through with the tree cork theory. In the middle of the work, Chief Charles Daxton ordered some pizzas and two liters of Pepsi to keep their energy up. Chief Charles Daxton called Mr. Andy Campbell to inform him of the task he and Lawrence were involved in. Besides, he expressed his intention of keeping and having Lawrence work for him. He found the inmate very interesting, outgoing and fun to be around. He was even ready to file a motion with the Fulton County District Attorney to have Mr. Jackson work for the Charlotte Police Department if everything went well. He got favorable consent from the high prison chief of Onslow Jail who couldn't but agreed. Chief Charles Daxton took Lawrence home after work and gave him the basement of his three-bedroom house on the outskirts of Charlotte. The basement entrance looked like a gym with all kinds of fitness equipment neatly arranged, and it had a large room reserved for family guests. The room was well furnished with double doors refrigerator full of orange juice, a variety of soda, cheese, water, milk, and fruits. A queen size bed in a corner covered with a sparkly clean white sheet with four pillows well arranged by the headboard. A bright 82" TV on the wall powered by a WiFi system that served the whole house no matter where someone was. The carpet in the room was soft and clean, where dirt had no place. A large glass window on the side of the large room in the basement allowed the dweller to enjoy a nice view of the backyard. A large bathroom with a sliding glass door was inside the room, taking away from the guest in the basement the need of going outside. Lawrence was shocked when Mr. Daxton presented him with the basement room and told him to feel at home. He was still admiring the room when Mr. Daxton brought his wife and two daughters to the basement to meet their new guest. The Chief Detective presented him as a new associate in the Charlotte Police Department, with whom he had a vital role the following day. Lawrence shook the hand of the wife and the two children thinking about his daughter Grace, who was about the same age as the Chief's daughters. They left Lawrence whose mind was on the beautiful times he had with his daughter in College Park, Georgia. When the Chief Detective drove home with Lawrence, he opened the garage door inside his car and entered the kitchen with a door leading down to the basement. Lawrence didn't have the chance to tour the house until dinner time when the Chief took him up from the basement. He was overwhelmed by the beauty around the Chief Detective's house, especially the golden automatic fireplace that controlled the house's temperature.

Chapter 15

Lawrence conquered his freedom.

Lawrence slept through the night as a baby because of the re-found comfort he lost for many years in incarceration. Mr. Daxton was up early for his morning workout in the basement while his guest was still sleeping. They woke Lawrence up around 7:00 a.m. to shower and join the breakfast table for a new day at his new job. He quickly bathed, put on his suit, and joined Mr. Daxton and his family at a dining room table. On the table, that morning was everything Lawrence longed for in a breakfast in his entire life. There was scrambled egg, bacon, sausage, cheese, yogurt, milk, oatmeal, whole-wheat waffle, avocado, apple, grapes, bananas, coffee, tea, and orange juice. After a short prayer, the children started eating cereal while Lawrence was still looking around the table, not knowing where to start. He got a hot, freshly brewed coffee in a cup, added some milk, and grabbed loaves of whole-wheat waffles. He enjoyed the vibe and the chemistry in the Daxton family, which he hoped for in the future.

Mrs. Daxton took her two daughters to school while the Chief Detective and his guest hopped on his white

Cadillac Escalade and drove to work. Lawrence and the Chief Detective resumed their task from the previous day, sorting the Unsolved Cold Cases of the Charlotte Police Department. They were supposed to thoroughly review those cases and identify the ones that occurred near a tree. By noon, they finally put their hands on five of those files, among which three were pretty in the time frame of the cork theory, meaning less than a year old. They assigned a particular file cabinet for the five unsolved criminal cases to reactivate them and get justice for the victims' families. They reorganized the files that didn't meet the criteria back to their respective file cabinet and quickly met to proceed with what they found. Around noon the two men went back to the Chief Detective's office. Lawrence retrieved the transparent container from the dark closet and laid it on the office desk. Finally, he requested a stack of printing papers to collect the images yielded in the container's liquid.

Lawrence folded two diagonal corners of the pile of printing papers and dropped them gently, one by one, on the surface of the liquid. He put the wet printing papers in the dark closet in the order in which he wetted them under the monitoring eyes of the Chief Detective. Lawrence closed well the dark closet to let the papers dry, and the two men went to their lunch break around 12:30 p.m. for an hour. Mr. Daxton and Lawrence walked three blocks from the police station to an Apple Bee restaurant for lunch. They both had a salad, well-done steak, French fries, mashed potato, gravy, and Sprite for drink.

At the end of the meal, Mr. Daxton handed the waitress his credit card while Lawrence asked himself how he would pay for this wonderful lunch. Back in the police facility,

Mr. Daxton introduced Lawrence to the Police Chief, Mr. Christopher Miller, who had a long meeting in the morning with his staff. Mr. Daxton expressed his desire to put Lawrence on the payroll and have the police department file a motion to the Fulton County District Attorney's office for temporary release. Mr. Daxton discussed the great benefit the Charlotte Police Department would gain from having Mr. Lawrence Jackson in his department. Without a promise from the Police Chief, a man of few words, the two men returned to Mr. Daxton's office. Around 4:00 p.m., Lawrence opened the dark closet to collect the dry printing papers, which revealed clear pictures of animals and people who got close to the tree on Main Street (NC-55). Upon seeing all these images, Mr. Daxton called the Chief Police to his office to witness the incredible discovery. Under his rolling eyes, Lawrence illuminated the irrelevant pictures and pointed to the photographs related to the young boy's case. The images revealed that a young woman in her middle twenties dropped the dark plastic bag under the tree on Main Street, Bayboro, North Carolina. What a break, the three men were hugging one another in disbelief of being one step closer to bringing justice for an innocent child.

Mr. Daxton and Lawrence promised the Chief Police to return to Bayboro the next day to look for the woman who committed this horrific act against the boy. Mr. Christopher Miller hired Lawrence on the spot and filed a motion to the Fulton County District Attorney to release Mr. Lawrence Jackson to the care of the Charlotte-Mecklenburg Police. Mrs. France Williams, the Fulton County DA, set a date to bring Mr. Lawrence Jackson back to court with a representative of the Charlotte Police Department for the release. The Chief

Detective agreed freely to take Lawrence back to Georgia to meet with Judge David Wallace and the Fulton County District Attorney to finalize the transfer into his custody. Before Police Chief Christopher Miller left for the day, he gave Mr. Lawrence Jackson his police badge and identification number. He also promised that the police department would pay for deposit money and the first month's rent for Lawrence to get an apartment in Charlotte. Mr. Charles Daxton was on the phone with his long-time friend Mr. Andy Campbell, the high prison chief at the Onslow Prison, to inform him of the decision of the Charlotte Police Department to keep Mr. Lawrence Jackson as an employee. Mr. Andy Campbell was pleased to vacant Lawrence's prison cell and put his books and belongings in storage until he requested them. Lawrence couldn't believe what was happening because everything was coming to him so fast without his control. It seemed to him like someone was working behind the scenes on his behalf without asking for his approval. The Chief Detective and his new associate drove home talking and laughing all alone, very happy about the day's accomplishment. When they got home, the Chief Detective opened his two cars garage from the dashboard and closed it back as soon as the vehicle stopped. As they exited the garage, Lawrence went to the basement, passed the fitness equipment, and opened his guest room door. He realized the room was cleaned, and the bed was made adequately with rearranged pillows. The bedsheet was changed, the socks on the floor got picked up, and the remote control was put back in its original location. Lawrence felt ashamed of himself for his negligence and said, "I just came out of prison, and I couldn't keep up with the orders in this house." The Daxton family and their guest ate and chatted at the dinner table until 9:00 p.m. when the kids were supposed to go to bed. Lawrence returned to his basement room, watched more TV, and didn't want to sleep in the bed. Lawrence couldn't wake up on time the following day and had to rush through the shower and the morning sophisticated breakfast.

At work, the Chief detective briefly met with his crew members and presented the new team member, Lawrence Jackson, with whom he would return to Pamlico County. All the crew members were aware of the findings to bring the young boy's case alive and the contribution of Lawrence's cork theory. After the meeting, the Chief Detective and Lawrence drove in a police officer marked car to Bayboro, showing the picture of the lady who jumped a child's body under the tree. They were confident of getting a break because Bayboro had less than two thousand people, and the probability of finding the lady was high. In every business they visited showing a clear picture of the lady, people admitted seeing the lady before but didn't know where she lived. Detective Charles Daxton and Lawrence Jackson went to the Wells Fargo Bank on Main Street, where their efforts paid off. Every teller in the bank knew the lady, for she was a regular customer who came in every Monday to deposit cash money into her checking account. At the request of the detectives, the bank manager pulled the lady's file to find her address and active phone number. The lady's name was Tracey Clayton, and she lived in the Bay River Apartment Complex a few miles from the Wells Fargo Bank. Bay River Apartment Complex was a lovely 20-unit garden apartment complex off NC Highway 55 on Fairview Court in Bayboro. The two detectives drove to the complex and knocked at the apartment: one Fairview Court, #8, Bayboro, NC 28515-9003. Miss Tracey Clayton opened the door, and the two detectives summoned her to the Charlotte police station the following Monday at 10:00 a.m. for a matter that concerned her. The detectives couldn't disclose much about the case against her despite her insistence to know more. They left Bayboro and headed back to Charlotte; happy to get this case solved by the coming Monday. On their way back, they decided not to tackle the five other unsolved criminal cases they created a separate file cabinet for. They wanted to deal with these cases with extreme care and diligently one after one to avoid confusion. As soon as they entered the Police Department, the Chief Police and the police lawyer cheerfully waited for them in the facility lobby. They were ushered into Chief Christopher Miller's office to have private concertation and review some procedures into Lawrence's case. The Fulton County District Attorney's Office set up a personal hearing for Mr. Lawrence Jackson's release on Wednesday at 10:00 a.m. at the county courthouse. Counselor Lilian Greene, the attorney for the Charlotte Police Department, was compelled to represent the department at this critical hearing. Chief Detective Charles Daxton wouldn't back down on his engagement to take Lawrence to this vital hearing of his life. Chief Daxton took the occasion to expand on Mr. Lawrence Jackson's crucial role in the investigation department. He would be a tremendous access to the department with a mastered cork theory that could revolutionize investigation procedures. They all decided to take Mr. Daxton's white Cadillac Escalator to Georgia on Wednesday morning and bring Lawrence back as a free man. They all were happy and laughing, hoping for a favorable outcome.

Mss. Tracey Clayton made it to her appointment on Monday at 10:00 a.m. at the Charlotte Police facility. She registered in the facility lobby, and a police officer took her to the interrogation room and waited for the Chief Detective. The interrogation room was a little room with a central table, two chairs, and a hidden central surveillance camera that recorded all the motions in the tiny space. Two police officers were in the surveillance room watching Tracey Clayton as Lawrence Jackson entered the interrogation room and displayed images of the crime scenes before her. As soon as Lawrence exited the room, Mss. Clayton put her two hands over her opened mouth to suppress her utterance. When Mr. Daxton came into the interrogation, he sat across from Mss. Tracey Clayton, whose eyes were in tears. In less than five minutes of interrogation, Mss. Clayton confessed to the involuntary murder of her one-year-old child. She made a chilly account of her son's death on a statement sheet.

Mss. Tracey Clayton lived with her mother in Charlotte in a one-bedroom apartment and worked in the strip club as a server. Her mother disapproved of her job and wanted her to find decent employment, but the young lady wouldn't listen because of the money. The relation mother and daughter got worsened, and Tracey decided to move out and stay far away from her mother. She worked only Friday through Sunday, made enough money to sustain herself, and needed no one to monitor her life. She rented an apartment at one Fairview Court, #8, Bayboro, NC 28515, where she lived happily, inviting all her male and female friends over. Soon after, Tracey became unexpectedly pregnant and didn't know the father of the baby in her belly. She was devasted but resumed her stripping job after the birth of her son, Michael. On weekends, Tracey would leave her son with her mother and work at the strip club until Sunday afternoon. She would pick up Michael and drive back to Bayboro. Every Monday morning, Tracey would deposit a lot of cash money in her Wells Fargo Bank account for her needs. When the boy was growing up, he would refuse to sleep in his crib and climb into her mother's bed at night. One night, Tracey was very drunk after having a horrible weekend at work, and Michael climbed again into her bed. In the middle of the night, Tracey slept on her son without realizing that her son was in her bed. In the morning, she realized the boy had no life in him, and she panicked and didn't know what to do. She tried CPR. It didn't work. She wanted to call the police, but she was scared the police would incriminate her. She decided to get rid of the body and dumped it in a bush somewhere far from her apartment. She thought a tiny brush on the other side of the Wells Fargo Bank would be a perfect hiding place to dump the dead body. Tracey Clayton signed the declaration but was troubled by her pictures at the time she left the boy corps in the brush. She wanted to know if a hidden camera was in the bush where she dumped her son Michael's body. The detective couldn't explain the origin of the pictures and showed that Tracey Clayton was in the same outfit coming to the interrogation as when she got rid of her son's body. The Chief Detective cuffed Ms. Tracey Clayton and said:" You are under arrest for the death of your child. You have the right to remain silent, and anything you say can be used against you in court. You have the right to an attorney. If you cannot afford an attorney, one will be provided. Do you understand the rights I have just read to you? Do you wish to speak to me with these rights?". He brought in a nurse to perform a buccal swab DNA collection on Ms. Tracey Clayton, who was speechless and overwhelmed by the situation in the interrogation room. The nurse put the DNA test kit on the table before Tracey Clayton and told her to stand up for a safe procedure. Tracey, who at that moment seemed to be absent of the spirit and was obeying every order she was being given without thinking or questioning it. With the swab between her forefinger and thumb, the nurse inserted the brush into one side of Tracey's mouth between the inside of the cheek and the upper gum. She pressed firmly and twirled the cheek brush against the inside of the inner cheek using an up-and-down motion from front to back and back to front. She used a stopwatch to time the collection procedure for at least thirty seconds per swab to recuperate as much buccal cells. She avoided saturating the swab with excess saliva and returned the swab carefully to the original container and closed the lid. She took the sample to the police crime lab for DNA testing. The Chief Detective took Ms. Tracey Clayton back to the police lobby to start the incarceration process, and he showed Lawrence Jackson how the inmate booking worked, and the paperwork required. He wanted to ensure that the suspect could appear before a judge in the next forty-eight hours.

The two detectives, delighted at their accomplishments, went down to the basement of the police station, where they kept the unsolved cold case files. They went through the five complex cases and decided to tackle the Case# 32-45, which occurred less than a year ago. Case# 32-45 involved a school principal who was adopted at gunpoint after she locked the school building and the access to the school parking lot. Her car was abandoned on a roadside, and her body was found three days after the FBI joined in the search for principal Chavez Atkinson. She was the Lucas Middle School principal in Durham, North Carolina, for over twelve years and was greatly supported by faculty and students. The policy and the FBI couldn't find out why someone would like to find Mss. Chavez Atkinson murdered. She was a people person, and she loved her students for whom she would do anything to help them succeed academically. The kidnapper drove her fifteen miles from the Lucas Middle School ground to the wood of the Duke Forest. The police didn't find a piece of DNA element on the body, but a fingerprint in the principal's vehicle that they believed might belong to the kidnapper. The police ran the fingerprint through the national database, but there was no successful match. After two months of trying unsuccessfully to find the kidnapper, the principal Chavez Atkinson's case went cold. The Chief Detective and Lawrence Jackson believed they could get a picture of the killer since the principal's body was left in the wood. The victim was shot two times in the head in executive style and abandoned in Duke Forest with her work clothes on. The body wasn't sexually assorted, giving a reason to believe an act of vengeance or retaliation.

Within two days, Tracey Clayton's DNA test result came out, and she was the biological mother of the boy Michael. She pleaded guilty to manslaughter and received a five-year prison sentence with a possibility of parole after three of incarceration. She refused to pay for her attorney, and the state of North Carolina provided her with an attorney during her court appearances. Tracey Clayton's case caught the local news outlets' attention. For many weeks, news outlets re-counted the story of Tracey Clayton and advice to all parents with small children. On their front pages, some newspapers displayed the picture of Tracy Clayton at the interrogation table and her image at the crime scene. Some other newspapers celebrated the dedicated work of the detectives at the Charlotte Police Department, which had a high approval rating. The tree cork theory the Department started using wasn't made public to the population of North Carolina.

Chapter 16

Lawrence made it to the rank of FBI agents

Wednesday early morning, the attorney Lilian Greene, Chief Detective Charles Daxton, and Lawrence Jackson met at the Chief's home by 6:00 a.m. and took the Chief's white Cadillac Escalade. The morning was tranquil, and the air still smelled fresh, but then slowly, the first rays of the sun peaked over far distant mountains, and everything gradually bathed in a foggy, golden light. There was less traffic on highway 87, and they hadn't yet crossed the North Carolina boundaries with South Carolina. Longtime memories of his beautiful times on the South Carolina beaches flashed through the Chief Detective's mind. He told his passengers how fabulous Folly Beach was, especially in summer. It was a beautiful stretch of beach with a giant pier, lighthouse, and plenty of unique shops and seafood restaurants. The restaurants offered a variety of seafood with a specialty of a fresh steamed bucket of blue crabs or shrimp glazed in delicious sauces. On their ride through South Carolina, they could enjoy the spectacular mountain views, pottery shops, and fishing spots where people could come and fish. When they crossed Northern Georgia, they could admire the Blue Ridge Mountains chain stretched as far as eyes could see. The uniqueness of this area of the south was its wineries, where they could visit some wine groves in some breathtaking valleys. Much of the valleys were bucolic and beautiful, especially in early summer when its small hills glowed in wildflowers. When they were getting closer to Atlanta, they could see Downtown Atlanta suddenly emerged and showered by abundant sun rays. It was an unforgettable road trip for all of them because there were a lot of new places to discover and new things to learn. They drove happily for about four hours to the Fulton County District Court, where they had an appointment with the District Attorney at 10:00 in the morning. They presented their police badges in the courthouse lobby, and a court clerk walked them into a small courtroom where the assistant District Attorney, John Welch, was waiting at the door. They all had a quick introduction and quickly went over their request on behalf of Lawrence Jackson, and they all went into the courtroom. They sat for about ten minutes when the Honorable Judge David Wallace emerged from a little door at a corner of the courtroom. After a presentation of Lawrence's team one by one, Judge David Wallace presided over the motion the Charlotte Police Department sent to the Fulton County District Attorney's Office. The judge granted the request with a restriction that Lawrence could work and live freely in North Carolina; any activities beyond the latter's boundaries would be considered a violation of the court order. Mr. John Welch requested a monitoring bracelet put on Lawrence Jackson's ankle for the court to monitor his whereabouts. The attorney Lilian Greene objected to using an ankle bracelet which would jeopardize the brilliant work of Mr. Lawrence Jackson. Chief Detective Charles Daxton intervened to explain to the judge the delicateness of Mr. Lawrence Jackson's responsibility with the Charlotte Police Department.

Moreover, he argued that using an ankle bracelet was unnecessary because instead would cause harm to their detective works. The two parties finally agreed to release Lawrence Jackson to the care of the Charlotte Police Department with the modality of serving only the state of North Carolina. A copy of the decision was given to Assistant District Attorney John Welch and one to the attorney Lilian Greene by Judge David Wallace, who kept a copy for the court record. Judge David Wallace ended the session, and the two parties went their separate ways after congratulating Mr. Lawrence Jackson. When they all left the courthouse and walked toward the white Cadillac Escalator, they all felt hungry simultaneously, as if someone had reminded them that they didn't eat the whole morning.

Lawrence proposed an I-Hop to get some mouth-watering southern food and warm hospitality. They ate and drank to celebrate their success until 12:30 p.m. when they started their journey back in the white Cadillac Escalade. When they got to the Chief Detective's Charlotte residence, Lawrence hugged the attorney Lilian Greene hard for a job well done before she got in her car and drove home. The next day at the Charlotte Police Department, Lawrence was met with the biggest surprise of his entire life. Police Chief Christopher Miller handed him a check for a month's salary and took him to his new apartment, where he put down a security deposit and a month's rent on behalf of Lawrence. The one-bedroom apartment was within walking distance from the police department's building, and Lawrence wouldn't need transportation to come to work every morning. The apartment was empty, and Lawrence had to furnish it and provide for his first necessities. The leasing manager was lovely and took Lawrence and Mr. Miller on a tour of the apartment complex to show the new resident his privileges and duties. The complex had a well-equipped gymnasium where the residents exercised every morning before work. The complex management hired a personal trainer who regularly trained residents on the gymnasium's various fitness equipment. A big summing pool in the back of the complex functioned from spring through summer. It also always had a summing coach who regularly taught children how to swim and have fun in the swimming pool. Lawrence was very excited about his new place of habitation and the community in which he would live. Most importantly, nobody in the neighborhood knew about his past, and he could easily blend in far away from College Park, Georgia. Police Chief Christopher Miller co-signed the lease agreement for Lawrence, and he received the keys to his new apartment and a mailbox key. So, all happy and smiling, Lawrence went with the Chief back to the police department to resume his daily activities.

Lawrence went to the police department basement, where Chief Detective Charles Daxton awaited him before an open folder. He was re-educating himself about the circumstances around the death of the Lucas Middle School principal, Chavez Atkinson. The two men in the basement studied the crime scene photos to determine the closest tree to Ms. Chavez Atkinson's dead body. The two detectives read the transcript of the death of Ms. Chavez Atkinson and reviewed the interrogation recording of the suspects in the case. The following day, the two detectives went to Duke Forest with the crime scene pictures to relocate where the victim's body was found. Chief Detective Charles Daxton managed to pinpoint the location where Ms. Chavez Atkinson's body was found. Lawrence removed his cutting instruments from his tool back and carefully cut the cork of the closest tree to the crime scene. The tree cork was placed in a clear zipper bag and taken to the police department, where Lawrence prepared a new magnesium chloride solution. He prepped the tree cork in the solution and added red vinegar to emerge the wood for twenty-four hours in a dark room. Noon time the next day, Lawrence and Charles Daxton were excited to collect pictures of people and animals who ever went by their targeted tree. When the printing papers dried, Lawrence and Charles Daxton went through the photos to eliminate the ones irrelevant to the case. Then, toward the end of the stack of pictures, they were lucky to find a photo of Ms. Chavez Atkinson kneeling and the gunman behind her. Charles Daxton took a picture of the gunman and ran it through the police database of criminals' photographs in North Carolina. There was a perfect match. It was the picture of a prison bird named Dwayne Carson, who just came out of jail on probation at the time of the crime. It took two days for the detectives to find a working number of Dwayne Carson, who was still living with his son Gregory in Durham. When he found his number, Chief Detective Charles called Dwayne Carson to schedule an interrogation the following day at Charlotte Police Department. Dwayne Carson affirmed he had nothing to do with Ms. Chavez Atkinson's case but would gladly respond to the invitation to the police station the following day. The same day, Lawrence and Charles presented the situation to the state judge Carl Jameson to secure a warrant to search Dwayne Carson's resident for the gun used to kill Ms. Chavez Atkinson. The next day at

10:00 a.m. Dwayne Carson showed up at the police station while Chief Detective Charles sent several police officers to Dwayne's residence to search for the pistol that killed Ms. Chavez Atkinson. A police officer walked Dwayne to the interrogation room, where he was videotaped and observed. A few minutes later, Lawrence Jackson came to the room; he displayed pictures of Dwayne Carson's presence at the crime scene before him and left the room. Mr. Dwayne Carson was shocked to see his photos of the day he was in Duke Forest with Mss. Chavez Atkinson holding his gun. First, he tried to hide the pictures, realized that wasn't a good idea and then stacked the photos in one pile. He was sweating heavily when Chief Detective Charles Daxton entered the interrogation room and drew his seat close to Dwayne Carson.

"We know what has happened between you and Ms. Chavez Atkinson in Duke Forest. Can you tell me how it went down?" the Chief Detective introduced the discussion.

By the time Dwayne Carson opened his mouth to start his confession, the Chief Detective had received a phone call from the police officers who went to Dwayne Carson's residence. They found two pistols under a pillow on Dwayne Carson's bed in his master room. The two guns were collected for forensic analysis; the bullets found in the victim's body during the autopsy were a perfect match. At that news, Dwayne Carson confessed to killing the Lucas Middle School principal, Ms. Chavez Atkinson. Dwayne Carson attended a parent-teacher conference with Ms. Chavez Atkinson at the Lucas Middle School, where his son Gregory attended. Mr. Dwayne Carson was a very handsome, tall man, and the parent-teacher conference turned into a meeting of mutual interest.

After discussing the ways to improve Gregory's academic performance, the two adults exchanged phone numbers in front of the minor. Ms. Chavez Atkinson was very interested in Dwayne Carson, and both set up a date on a Friday afternoon after school. For the date, Dwayne Carson came in a black Mercedes to pick up the Lucas Principal at her house. He took her to a restaurant in the UNC Charlotte Marriott Hotel, where they ate, drank, and had a good time. From the Marriott Hotel lobby, Dwayne and Chavez got on a cab that took them to the lake beach of Lake Norman, where they had a pleasant walk and laughed about silly things. The taxi took them back to the hotel. They drove to the AMC Carolina Pavilion on 9541 South Boulevard, Charlotte, North Carolina, for a romantic movie that ended around 7:00 p.m. Dwayne Carson spent a lot of money on Ms. Chavez that evening to have an unforgettable event with his date. At the end of the evening, Dwayne Carson proposed to take Ms. Chavez home for the weekend.

Ms. Chavez objected to Dwayne's advance and argued that it was just the first date and was looking for more dates to get to know him deeply. Dwayne became uncontrollably angry, his face turned red, and his two eyes were about to leave their orbit. Ms. Chavez realized this man needed an anger management class and calmly asked to be dropped off at home. On Ms. Chavez Atkinson's porch, the two hugged one another for a quick moment and promised to call for the next date. Two days later, Dwayne Carson was arrested for drug possession with the intention of distribution. He spent about a year in jail thinking about Ms. Chavez every day, hoping to marry her one day after he got out of jail. Meanwhile, Ms. Chavez moved on and found another school assistant principal in her county who proposed to her. Finding out that Dwayne had an anger management issue was a turn-off for Ms. Chavez, who decided in her heart not to see him again. Two days after he got out of jail, Dwayne went to the Lucas Middle School at closing to re-ignite his love for the principal. The rejection from the lady he had been dreaming about for a year in his prison cell was unbearable and unacceptable. When Ms. Chavez showed him her new engagement ring, a feeling of "if I couldn't have her, no one should have her" came upon him. Three days later, on a Monday afternoon at school closing, Dwayne Carson went to the school ground and abducted the principal at gunpoint. He forced her to drive her car to Duke Forest, where he shot her in the back of her head after making her kneel by a tree. He abandoned Ms. Chavez Atkinson's car on the roadside and called a UBER to take him home.

After signing the confection paper, Chief Detective Charles Daxton placed Dwayne Carson under arrest. He put him in the Charlotte Police Department Jail while awaiting a criminal trial. Just a day later, the forensic result of the two guns collected from Dwayne's house and sent to the FBI crime lab in Virginia came out. There was a perfect match between the two bullets retrieved from the head of the Lucas Middle School Principal and one of the two guns seized from Dwayne's bedroom. Evidence against Dwayne in the court proceeding was overwhelming, and no attorney was willing to take on his case. Instead, he was assigned a public defender whose insanity argument didn't convince the jury, who unanimously found the defender guilty on all counts. The jury believed that the defender premeditated all his actions and planned them diligently to satisfy his anger over losing somebody he loved. Dwayne was given thirty years in federal prison for kidnapping and murdering a school principal. Many national news outlets were interested in the case and broadcasting all the different steps in the case of the loving and caring Lucas Middle School principal's murder. CNN and Fox telecasted the 12 jurors' decision to convince Mr. Dwayne Carson, praising the Charlotte Police Department's investigation abilities.

The case caught the attention of the FBI Director, Max Richardson, who was very interested in Lawrence Jackson's work. Mr. Max Richardson called Chief Police Christopher Miller in Charlotte, North Carolina, to request that he send Mr. Lawrence Jackson to see him in his 934 Pennsylvania Avenue NW, Washington, DC office. He had already purchased a plane ticket from Charlotte Douglas International airport to the Reagan National Airport. He would fly with Southwest Airlines, and Secret Service Agents would be waiting for him at the departure area on the upper level. They would bring him to his office for an opportunity of his lifetime. Mr. Max Richardson sent an electronic plane ticket to the Police Chief on behalf of Lawrence Jackson. Mr. Christopher Miller called Lawrence Jackson to his office, broke the news, and gave him the electronic plane ticket with all the instructions. Two Secret Service Agents were at the aircraft door the following Monday before Lawrence got out of the plane that just landed. They verified his ID and police badge number and took him to FBI Director Max Richardson's office to meet with him. Mr. Max Richardson was thrilled to see him and allowed him to expose his tree cork theory. Lawrence Jackson explained in detail how the tree cork theory functioned and the cases he solved to put criminals behind bars. Mr. Max Richardson saw a big help in Lawrence, and he called his secretary to arrange his trip to the FBI crime lab in Quantico, Virginia. After less than fifteen minutes, the secretary returned to inform Mr. Richardson that his ride was ready. When the two men reached the bottom of the building, where Mr. Richardson's office was, there was a brand-new black Chevrolet Tahoe. One FBI agent opened the vehicle's passenger door for the director and Lawrence to hop on board. For about 1 hour 30, they pulled to the FBI crime lab's parking lot in Quantico, and Mr. Richardson and Lawrence Jackson took the elevator to the eighth floor. A thousand of cabinets on the eighth floor contain all the FBI unsolved murder cases nationwide. Mr. Richardson explained his desire to open a Tree Cork Unit on the seventh floor, where he wanted to appoint Lawrence Jackson as Chief of the division where many qualified agents would work for him. Lawrence would assign duties to those working for him to go through the unsolved case files and identify the ones that occurred in the presence of a tree. The department would create plastic containers in the Tree Cork Unit, filled with a magnesium chloride solution. The FBI director, Mr. Max Richardson, asked Lawrence if he would like to take on this responsibility. Lawrence Jackson accepted the job offer and evoked the boundaries the Fulton County District Attorney's Office imposed on him. On the spot, Mr. Max Richardson called his secretary in DC to instruct her to have the Fulton County District Attorney Office to extradite Mr. Lawrence Jackson's case. After the deal concluded and warm hands shook, the two men jumped back in the brand-new Chevrolet Tahoe and drove to Washington, DC. Mr. Max Richardson had Lawrence sign many documents referring to his engagement to dedicate his life to serving the judiciary branch of the government. Then Mr. Richardson ushered Lawrence to a lounge room on his floor where a team of chefs served food and beverage. Lawrence was presented as a new addition to the FBI corporation to help the justice department fight crimes. In Quantico, a fully furnished apartment reserved for people in the witness protection program was given to Lawrence. A badge that read Chief of Cork Unit displaying Lawrence's photo ID was handed to him by the FBI director and an access code to the crime lab. Lawrence went through a week of orientation where he learned about the operation of the Justice Department and its components. He studied the role of the FBI agents and the hierarchy that governed them. Every morning FBI agent would come to his apartment in Quantico to take him to the orientation, after which he was offered a six-figure salary.

Chapter 17

Lawrence Jackson, an international detective

Lawrence Jackson, the Chief Cork Unit manager, reorganized the Cork Unit to maximize his productivity. The unit got two small rooms on the left. The first room received the "Dark Room" sign on the door, and the second one got the sign "Storage Room" printed on it. The dark room had shelves around the walls where Lawrence put plastic containers with a piece of cork merged in a magnesium chloride solution combined with red vinegar. He also used a cabinet to store the printing papers to collect images generated from the piece of cork. Lawrence was the only one authorized to go in the storage room wearing a night vision goggles. The second room was used to store sacs of magnesium powder, gallons of chloric acid, and bottles of red vinegar vital elements for the cork theory. People would find an empathetic scale Lawrence would use to weigh the magnesium powder on his desk. On the far right of the unit, he had ten file cabinets with five drawers. He labeled every single drawer with the name of all the fifty states of the United States of America. The Department of Justice hired two agents, Keith Ross and Cortez Gomez, who would work for the Chief Cork Unit Manager. The role of the two agents was to go through the cold case files on the eighth floor of the building and sort the ones that occurred around bushes or trees. Those files would be placed in the drawer of the state where the crime was committed.

Lawrence set up his performance so high to solve one new cold case every week. The two new agents, Keith Ross and Cortez Gomez, assisted him in everything and had assimilated very well the Cork theory. In his first two weeks, he tackled two FBI unsolved murder cases and turned the outcome to Mr. Max Richardson, who was very impressed with the work. In the third week, the German Chancellor called the White House to request the service of the FBI in a high-profile criminal case in Hamburg, Germany. The Chancellor promised to endorse the cost and pay for the travel expenses and the lodging of the agent who would come and help solve the crime. The Chancellor insisted they needed an agent with experience with the Cork Theory because the crime in Hamburg was committed under an apple tree. The following day, the FBI director Max Richardson was called to the White House and briefed on the request of the German Chancellor. The Cork Unit Chief, Lawrence Jackson, was designated to travel to Germany and helped solve the high-profile criminal case in Hamburg. In three days, Lawrence Jackson acquired his passport, plane ticket, and all he needed to complete the work. Two days later, the Cork Unit Chief packed his suitcase with his favorite suits and the main ingredients and equipment necessary for his job. He flew from the Dulles International Airport on Lufthansa Airlines for 8 hours and 45 minutes to the Hamburg Airport (Flughafen Hamburg). At the Hamburg Airport, a warm welcome was given to him by the state of Hamburg Chief Polizei, who came personally to greet him. He took Lawrence in a brand-new Mercedes to the Holiday Inn Hamburg, where a presidential suite was reserved. The front desk manager, Anke Schreiber, quickly processed his passport and ordered a room guest agent to take his luggage to the presidential suite. Lawrence was told to rest for the day, and in the morning, Chief Polizei would come to get him to meet the team working on the case. A few minutes after the departure of Chief Polizei, Anke Schreiber went to Lawrence's suite to explain all the benefits of the presidential suite. She was the only one on the hotel staff who spoke fluent English and could help Lawrence with his numerous questions. The next day, at 9:00 a.m., Chief Polizei came with his driver in the brand-new Mercedes to pick Lawrence Jackson up to the Bergedorf Police Department. Lawrence met with a team of three detectives who, for about two hours, went over the murder case with numerous crime scene pictures. Although there was a communication gap, the pictures clearly told the story of the crime. The case involved the Green Party leader, Anna Gunther, who was found dead in Wilhelm-Iwan-Ring, a small town in Hamburg, Germany.

Anna Gunther was a very dynamic leader of the Green Party in Germany. She fearlessly pushed the Green Party agenda in government policies and influenced schools and universities across Germany. Reducing green gas was at the center of Anna Gunther's battle against all the companies in Germany. The influence of the Green Party was constantly expanding throughout small towns and big cities. The party was growing in number and became the envy of some politicians and business owners. Anna Gunther was married to the director of a pharmaceutical company and was a mother of two children. They lived in Wilhelm-Iwan-Ring, a small town near Bergedorf, Hamburg. Mr. Gunther purchased a Tesla X model electric car for his wife, Anna, to avoid using fossil fuel as a model for all Germans to reduce the effect of greenhouse gases. Anna Gunther held different campaigns to educate the German populations on the impact and the danger of the greenhouse gases that were the primary cause of climate change. The unexpected flood and longer winter seasons in Germany lately were sign of the eminent threat. For her, the first step to combat this climate change was to stop using cars powered by fossil gas that ejected carbon dioxide into the earth's atmosphere.

The Green Party leader drove her Tesla X to the train station of Mittlerer Landweg and got on an S-Bahn for a meeting in the center of Hamburg. Anna was in a forum in Hauptbahnhof until 8:30 p.m. when she took the train back to the parking lot of the Mittlerer Landweg, where her car was parked. When she returned to open her car door, she found the vehicle handles taped. While trying to remove the tape, someone came out of nowhere to knock her on the ground with a heavy crowbar. Unconscious on the floor, the murderer tied an electric cord to her neck and strangled her to death. The killer took the lifeless body to the other side of the train tracks to hide it under an apple tree in front of an unoccupied cabin. The killer left without leaving a DNA trail because he was wearing gloves. The following day, the cabin owner came in to prepare and get ready his cabin for the summer, discovered the body, and called the police. The police came, took pictures of the scene, and realized that the Green Party leader was a victim of a lethal attack. The police locked down the cabin areas and took Anna Gunther's body to the University Medical Center Hamburg-Eppendorf for autopsy. The assassination of the Green Party leader was on the news for weeks, and her party members mourned her deeply. The national opinion condemned the vicious attack on the Green Party leader and called for an investigation and legal punishment for the perpetrator. Many organizations in the country bet money for the person who would help find and convince the killer.

After getting to know the case, Lawrence Jackson asked to be taken to the crime scene. He cut a big chunk of the apple tree cork before the sealed cabin, put it in a plastic bag, and requested Chief Polizei two days of work. In his hotel room, Lawrence prepared a magnesium chloride solution in a transparent plastic container where he added the cork and emerged it with red vinegar. He put the container in the closet of one of the two master bedrooms of the presidential suite, turned off all the lights, and went to the front desk to get the train map of Hamburg. The front desk manager proposed to take Lawrence to the Hamburg center after her shift ended, but Lawrence declined the offer. He didn't want people to know who he was and the purpose of his visit to Hamburg. He walked from his hotel to the Berliner Tor train station to enjoy the fresh spring flower aroma in the air. He purchased a one-day train ticket at a ticket dispenser machine before boarding a train to Hauptbahnhof. He sat by a window to contemplate the lovely view of the city. At Hauptbahnhof, Lawrence followed people going from department store to department store. He was overwhelmed by the numerous summer clothes on display and other accessories like suitcases, hats, shoes, belts, and much more. Lawrence was amazed by how people peacefully made transactions from train to walking from store to store. Some restaurants were between the department stores, and Lawrence spotted the sign of the number one American fast-food McDonald's at a distance. He walked to the McDonald's and opened the door to order a Big McMeal with French fry and a medium Pepsi. After his meal, the energy came upon him, and he could walk back to the train station. He went to the upper level of the Bahnof for a spectacular view of trains coming from different directions of Hamburg to drop off people and pick up other passengers to different city areas. As the night started, many restaurants at the top level of the Bahnof opened their doors for business. Lawrence decided to visit each restaurant to discover the variety of dishes offered to people and travelers through Hauptbahnhof. Lawrence was amazed to realize that cuisines worldwide were represented on the upper level of Hauptbahnhof. He sampled food from Marocain, Italian, Chinese, Turkish, and German cuisines. He had the wonderful experience of a lifetime and forgot all about time. When he realized that he needed to return to his hotel, it was almost midnight when the restaurants' bright lights were down, and the trains rarefied. The last train to Berliner Tor, the time for Lawrence to get to the lower level of the Bahnof, left the train station. At first, he panicked inside when he was told that the train operation would resume at 3:00 a.m. for the early passengers. But he learned he could call a cab to take him back to his hotel, a well-known inn in Hamburg. The taxi was a little pricy but dropped Lawrence at the Holiday Inn Hamburg with a charge of $40 on his credit card. He went up to his presidential suite, which was completely dark because the cork experiment was underway. Tired but happy about the day's self-enjoyment, he quickly took a warm shower and went to bed in the darkness. The next day, he woke up late, around noon, and would have to wait until 3:00 p.m. to open the dark closet and retrieve the transparent container with the cork solution. While Lawrence was thinking about what to eat, the front desk manager called him from the lobby to inquire why he didn't have breakfast and lunch. He explained to the lady that he had gone out the previous day and had a blast in the center city of Hamburg and came very late to the hotel. Anke Schreiber assured him that Hamburg had more fun places than the Hauptbahnhof, and she would voluntarily show him all. In addition, she promised to send his breakfast and lunch to the presidential suite because it was a part of the deal when the room was booked for Lawrence Jackson. The suite was a lavish 110 sqm two-bedroom, providing the ultimate luxurious living experience. Intended for a royal family, the spacious suite was furnished with top-quality furniture, ideal for an extravagant ambiance. The presidential suite was located on the hotel's top floor and fully equipped for the perfect lifestyle of distinguished guests. It featured a living room, a dining room, a kitchen, and two master bedrooms. The suite had a two-door refrigerator full of juice, soda, milk, cheese, croissant, bread, yogurt, champagne, fruits, and mineral water. Fifteen minutes after talking with the front desk manager, the hotel's assistant chef brought all kinds of food to Lawrence's dining room. He apologized numerous times while laying the food on the dining table. The front desk manager, Anke Schreiber, and the hotel staff knew Lawrence was a prestigious personality but didn't know who he was. Lawrence stayed in his hotel room until 3:00 p.m. when he retrieved the transparent container from the second bedroom closet. He called the front desk to request a stack of printing papers needed to collect the images released by the chunk of the apple tree cork. Anke Schreiber made the trip up in the elevator to hand the paper to Lawrence and realized the dirty plates and unfinished food on the dining table. She called the kitchen staff to remove the dirty plates and ordered housekeeping personnel to do a "stayover" cleaning of the suite before she exited the room. Before she left the room, she told Lawrence that her off day was coming up and she would be willing to take him to enjoy fun places in Hamburg. He accepted but didn't know he was making a mistake by accepting.

Lawrence folded two diagonal corners of the papers. He gently dropped them on the surface of the liquid on top of the cork in the transparent container to collect as many images released in the solution. He took the papers to dry them in the dark closet of the second bedroom until the morning.

Chapter 18

Lawrence Jackson solving crime in other countries

The next day, Lawrence woke up at 8:00 a.m. to start working on the project to unveil the image of the person who killed the Green Party leader, Anna Gunther. He opened the dark closet to bring to light the pictures of the printing papers he had let dry the previous day. He went through the photos individually to discard the ones irrelevant to the case he was working on. Lawrence was so happy to see the image of the killer that emerged clearly and simply with the dead body on his shoulder when laying it down under the apple tree. Lawrence called Chief Polizei Rudi, who, within fifteen minutes, came to take him to the Bergedorf Police Station, where the detective team was waiting anxiously. They went to a room of high confidentiality where Lawrence displayed photos of a six-foot-tall white man. The man was front head bold with a muscular body built who deposited the inert corps of Mrs. Anna Gunther by the apple tree and returned to bring a bedsheet to cover the body. The three detectives in the room revealed the bold-head man was a well-known car dealer in Bergedorf. He dealt with brand-new and used cars in Bergedorf, where many people came to buy vehicles from him.

Chief Polizei Rudi ordered two police officers to go to the man's place of business and bring him in handcuffs. The two police officers didn't find him at the location of his business, but his employees gave his home address to the officers. He was handcuffed in his home, in front of his wife and two kids, and brought to the Bergedorf police station. Handcuffed, sitting at a table in an interrogation room, Lawrence displayed all the photos of the man's involvement in the killing of the Green Party Leady. Overwhelmed by the evidence before him, Mr. Martin Dork admitted to the crime, and his motive was that Anna Gunther's fight against greenhouse gases and climate change was hurting his business. He stated that his car sales had decreased since the Green Party leader started her campaign, and many of his customers requested electric cars. Chief Polizei Rudi sent Martin to jail and made a short presentation to the local news outlets of ZDF in the presence of the three investigators. In his presentation, he assured the population of Hamburg that he had hands on the person who murdered Mr. Anna Gunther and was jailed, waiting for his trial.

Lawrence wasn't allowed to participate in the exhibition for possible retaliation and was dropped at his hotel at Berliner Tor. Chief Polizei Rudi and the three detectives were pleased about Lawrence's works leading to Martin Dork's incarceration. Chief Polizei Rudi personally invited Lawrence Jackson to dinner at his house before his return to the US. The news of the arrest of Martin Dork went vital throughout the state of Hamburg with much enthusiastic satisfaction and rejoicing that justice would be served. In the afternoon,

Lawrence took the train back to Hauptbahnhof to enjoy the ambiance of the center city of Hamburg again. He loved the place because he blended in a crowd where nobody knew him or asked him a question. He went from place to place, keeping his eye on the watch of his iPhone so that he could leave the area before the trains stopped running. The site became his favorite hangout spot, where he admired the connectivity between the different types of trains and even more with the bus system. The next day, Anke Schreiber took a day off and knocked at Lawrence's presidential suite at 11:00 a.m. to take Lawrence to a promenade of his lifetime. Lawrence Jackson was packing his clothes in a new suitcase he bought when Anke came in and sat at the dining table. Lawrence went to take a shower and dress up semi-casual for the occasion. The two friends left the presidential suite, took an elevator to the hotel's first floor, and walked to the Berliner Tor train station. They purchased the daily pass and waited on the train platform until a train going to the center city came. The two friends boarded one of the middle wagons and sat next to the other as a couple. Lawrence sat by the window to have a good view of all activities at every train station stop they were going through. On the other hand, Anke had her eyes on Lawrence's outfit with many questions running through her mind.

"Are you married, Lawrence?" Anke asked.

"I'm not married, but I have two children who live with their mother," he replied.

"Are you a rich person?" she continued.

"No, I'm not," he answered.

"Why do they book a presidential suite for you?" she inquired.

"I don't know. You can change it for a standard room, and it won't make a difference," he replied.

"It's stated in your passport that you're a government agent," she pursued.

"In the US, many people have contracts with the government. It doesn't mean they all are wealthy," he answered.

Anke Schreiber realized that Lawrence wasn't willing to talk about himself, and she stopped asking him many questions. She was admiring all his moves. They took the train to Hauptbahnhof, which was already booming with travelers going up and down. They went to the back of the Bahnof into a park where they admired different birds actively searching for food. Two old women were feeding the birds by throwing pieces of bread in the air. Lawrence and Anke took the U-Bahn to Jungfernstieg, the most beautiful shopping area in Hamburg. Various shopping windows exhibited high-quality clothes like jackets, suits, alligator shoes, belts, men's hats, and much more. From Jungfernstieg, they took the train to Reeperbahn, a city where freedom and perversion met. The little town of Reeperbahn was influenced by the British Rock and Roll stars of the 19th and 20th centuries, with many nightclubs where travelers came to let all loose.

Then the two friends hopped back on a S-Bahn to Altona, a city at the sea's edge with a mega train hub. Lawrence and Anke walked from the train station to the seashore to admire huge ships coming through Altona harbor. Lawrence was very fascinated by the organization of the city of Altona with a very sophisticated train system. Coming back to the train station, Anke took Lawrence to a gorgeous restaurant next to the train station in a glass building on the seventh floor. Anke had already made a reservation at the restaurant, where a table was set in a corner for two. She had pre-ordered the food and the drink for an unforgettable moment with the man her heart longed for. Lawrence and Anke ate and laughed about little things, and toward the end of their enjoyment, Anke laid her right hand on Lawrence's left hand. She was looking him straight in the eyes without talking. A feeling of enlightenment went through Lawrence, who started seeing the lady in front of him differently. He started noticing how pretty the lady was, with her well-defined hazel eyes and lips. Anke Schreiber was a charming young woman two years younger than Lawrence Jackson, who had never been married. She was an adorable creature with eyes perfectly framed by well-formed eyebrows. Her long sharp nose was well centered, creating an asymmetrical oval-shaped bulged face. Her jawline correctly exposed the lower edge of her face distinguishing it from her beautiful neck. The golden necklace she was wearing was shining in her face with an irresistible appeal Lawrence had never felt before. Her chest exhibited her breasts well preserved from sagginess and still holding firm. She was slim with the trim body of a model that showed her thin waistline and slender, shapely long legs. Lawrence grabbed Anke's two hands at the end of the dinner and drew her to himself when the lovers stood up to leave the restaurant.

Anke came so close to Lawrence that their noses were touching, and Lawrence made a move onto Anke's lips. The two lovers started violently kissing one another with passion and emotion. They left the restaurant together, holding hands, walking to the Altona train station, and got on a S-Bahn toward Bergedorf. They sat beside one another, and Lawrence put his arm around Anke's neck to keep her warm body against his left side. On the train, they kissed some more before reaching the Berliner Tor train station, where Lawrence got off the train and Anke continued to Bergedorf. She promised to come and see him first thing in the morning. Anke wanted to make sure she had the approval of her parents, who were somehow conservative and unpredictable sometimes. The next day, Anke Schreiber reported to work and told the hotel's general manager that she wasn't feeling well. She went up to stay with Lawrence. The two lovers spent a whole day together to know more about each other and to be intimate. Anke ordered from the presidential suite a breakfast from the hotel kitchen, and she reorganized the suite and sent dirty clothes to the laundry. She also reorganized the bed area and clothes in Lawrence's suitcase. At noon, Anke Schreiber ordered lunch on behalf of Lawrence, and they ate and laughed about all the little things. They learned more about each other and enjoyed themselves in their new life together, which had just begun. They laughed when Chief Polizei Rudi knocked at the presidential suite door to take them for dinner in his house. Lawrence and Anke packed everything that belonged to Lawrence and locked the suite to ride with Chief Polizei Rudi to his house. When they got to the Chief's house, a long white table was dressed and covered with different dishes new to Lawrence.

Anke was serving as an interpreter between the Chief's family and Lawrence. The Chief had a wife and three children who didn't speak nor understand English but wanted to show their gratitude for Lawrence's work. Chief Polizei Rudi testified how highly pleased was the German Chancellor to know that the criminal was under arrest. The Chancellor told Chief Polizei to inform Lawrence that he would send a messenger to the White House. Lawrence and Anke had a good time with the Chief's family until 7:00 p.m., when Lawrence was supposed to report at the airport for his return flight to the Dulles International Airport. The separation between Lawrence and Anke was very emotional. They both were crying, hugging, and kissing. Lawrence didn't want to leave Anke, who didn't want to let him go. Lawrence was the last passenger to board the Lufthansa Aircraft in a feeling of agony. His heart was thorned into two, and anger overcame him during the 8 hours 45 flight back to the US.

At the exit of the Dulles International Airport Hall, Lawrence called an Uber that dropped him at his apartment door angry and lonely. The next day, he went to Washington, DC, FBI headquarter to meet with Mr. Max Richardson to give an account of his mission to Hamburg, Germany. The FBI director was very impressed with the success of Lawrence Jackson's involvement in investigations worldwide. Then he returned to the FBI forensic crime laboratory in Quantico, Virginia, to resume his work. His two associates were on task to fill all the cabinets at the Cork Unit with unsolved cases near a tree from all the fifty states of the US. They studied every case to determine how high the possibility of solving the "cold case" was. They put the files into three categories: high possibility, medium possibility, and low possibility. A week later, after he returned to the US, the German Chancellor sent his Foreign Affairs Minister to the White House. The Foreign Minister was carrying a check of $500,000, which was the money raised for the person who would help find and prosecute the Green Party leader's killer. The pharmaceutical company Mr. Gunther worked for gave $200,000; the Green Party raised $100,000, and the German government donated $200,000. Martin Dork was convicted by a professional judge and five lay judges and was sentenced to fifteen years in prison with hard work. After the conviction, the German government decided the prize money should go to the Cork Detective who cracked the case. The FBI Director Max Richardson was called to the White House and instructed to bring in the Chief Cork Detective, Lawrence Jackson. A prize check of $500,000 was handed to Lawrence, who became very emotional, with tears dripping down his two cheeks. Since it was a prize money the government wouldn't take tax out of the lump sum. Lawrence was asked what he wanted to do with that large amount of money, and he answered that he wanted to buy a house close to his job. The Executive Chief in the White House urged him to see the director of the Virginia Housing Authority to find him a great place to stay. After leaving the White House, Lawrence had a video chat with his girlfriend, Anke Schreiber, to break the news.

The two lovers were joyful, and Lawrence decided to buy a plane ticket for Anke to come and celebrate with him. Lawrence took a day off to take care of some personal business the next day and deposited the check in his account. From the bank, Lawrence went to meet with the Virginia Housing Development Authority in Richmond, Virginia. The housing agency could locate a tax lien property in Dumfries, only fifteen minutes from Quantico, Virginia. It was a decent property that accrued unpaid property taxes and penalties of

$80,000. The house featured a spacious living room, a large master room, two children's rooms, a breathtaking kitchen, and a swimming pool at the front. The house was built on a vast land appropriate for children playground or hosting barbeque gatherings in the summer. Lawrence decided to buy the home, wrote a check to cover all the expenses, and started the property acquisition process. In two weeks, the keys to the new house were given to Lawrence, who received a call from Anke Schreiber at Dulles International Airport. The two lovers were reunited in joy, and Lawrence took her to the new house since the apartment he was living in was meant for witness protection people. Anke pressed Lawrence to the Dumfries' City Hall to sign a marriage certificate to regularize her stay in the United States. Then she convinced Lawrence to join the Dumfries Baptist Church so they could have a decent marriage celebration amid a congregation.

Lawrence neglected spiritual values all his life, and they became the cornerstone of his home. Anke left behind her two parents and a younger sister Izabella who was very attached to her. They called Anke almost daily to check on her and inquired about her American lifestyle, which always amazed them. They all wanted to come when they learned Lawrence and Anke would tie the nod, but Anke vigorously opposed it. They bought a lot of newlywed gifts that they shipped to the couple's new house address in Dumfries. The Schreiber family was delighted to see the older daughter married in America. It was a kind of a dream come true. Anke and Izabella dreamt about going to America and starting a lucrative business in beauty or fashion while they were still young. But, growing up, they buried those childhood dreams and were confronted with everyday reality and life challenges. The two sisters had everything in common; this was the second time they came apart in a long distance. The first time was when Anke went to London to attend college. They used Skipe and WhatsApp applications to keep in touch with one another and talk about their parents' whereabouts. Some of Anke's friends and co-workers also were excited about her finding love in America and living the dream of her life. Some sent wishful postcards and customized wedding emojis for the wedding celebration. Her friends and co-workers loved and missed her dearly, for Anke was a bright morning star growing up in Bergedorf.

Chapter 19

Lawrence Jackson's visit to Georgia

A month after Lawrence and Anke signed the marriage certificate in the Dumfries' City Hall, they married in the Dumfries Baptist Church. The reception was held in Lawrence's new house, in the big backyard. Only people from the church and some FBI agents attended the celebration because Anke didn't want any grandiose celebration. Anke objected to Lawrence's decision to use his prize money for any lavish wedding reception in a big hotel. Anke Schreiber argued that Lawrence's income as an FBI agent was enough for the couple to have a decent marriage and a decent lifestyle without being in debt to anyone. A heated argument convinced Lawrence to accept buying a used but very dependable Nissan Murano for work. The prize money was secured in a Wells Fargo Bank, where the couple planned to borrow more money to build an apartment building in Arlington, Virginia. Lawrence called an appraisal agency to value his new house, and the appraisal agent certified the home's value at $400,000. The couple had an appointment with a Wells Fargo Bank loan officer to present the deed of the house and the prize money as collateral to secure a loan of eight million dollars. The Paramount Construction Company won the bid to build two hundred apartments on one hectare of land in Arlington, Virginia, for the Jacksons. Anke would manage the apartment building, while Lawrence would focus more on his crime-fighting work with the FBI. After her high school diploma in Hamburg, Anke went to Property Management School in London, which allowed her to become the front desk manager of the Holiday Inn of Berliner Tor, Hamburg. She had a passion for managing significant buildings.

A month after his wedding celebration, the British Prime Minister called the White House to request help from the FBI agents to solve a crime. The crime involved a well-known priest gunned down in a church on the outskirt of London. The church compound was closed to the public until the investigation was completed and the perpetrator found. The Prime Minister explained that he learned the FBI could get pictures from tree cork when a crime was committed around a tree. Trees surrounded the chapel where the murder was committed, and he was confident that the Cork Theory would help solve the crime. The British Government promised to endorse all the expenses the US Government would incur in sending a qualified FBI agent. Mr. Max Richardson was called to the White House and was presented with the British Prime Minister's request. Mr. Richardson took the mission ticket to Lawrence at the crime laboratory in Quantico, Virginia, and added a government credit card for all the expenses. Lawrence told his wife he was going to London for a week of mission to work solve a crime committed in a church on the outskirt of the city. Anke wouldn't let Lawrence go to London alone for many reasons she couldn't explain. First, she didn't want any British girl to win her husband's heart alone in the streets of London. Second, that was an occasion for her to visit her former classmates and instructors who helped her at the University of London. Lawrence and his wife, Anke, went to London to work on the priest James Knight's case to find his killer. London police officials received Lawrence and his wife with great expectation, showed them the pictures of the crime scenes, and took them to the church compound. Without wasting time, Lawrence went to work at once and focused on an oak tree at the entrance of the church compound. Lawrence found a white Volvo with license plate number 321AG that followed the priest shortly after he came to prepare for a Wednesday evening service. The London police traced the owner of the white Volvo, registered to a grad student, Matthew Walker. In search of his house, the police found the revolver used to kill the Anglican priest, James Knight. The London police arrested Matthew Walker, who confessed to killing the priest because James Knight had molested him once. Matthew Walker was convicted and sentenced to twenty years in prison. Anke took the opportunity to visit her former classmates and went shopping sprees in different London Malls. Anke took Lawrence, the last Saturday before they departed from the UK, to see her best friend, Priscilla Gordon, who was still living in the City of London with her husband and two sons. Anke and Priscilla met again after a long separation from the University of London, where the two friends studied together. They embraced one another for a long time, and Priscilla presented Anke and Lawrence to her family. On the other side, Anke introduced her husband, Lawrence Jackson, to Priscilla's husband and two sons. Priscilla turned the occasion into a big celebration where she ordered different dishes from the restaurant owned by her husband in the heart of the City of London. They drank and ate and chatted all day long. Priscilla's husband invited some good neighbors to join in the celebration. At the end of the feast, Priscilla and his husband drove their two guests to their hotel and wished them a safe trip back to America.

The ambiance and the enjoyment in Priscilla's house incited a discussion about Lawrence's two children, that were still living with their mother. Lawrence and Anke decided to bring Joshua and Grace to come and live with their father, who was financially secure to provide for them. Lawrence and Anke took a British Airline from the London International Airport to the Dulles Airport in Virginia the following day. When a cab driver dropped Lawrence and Anke at their new house in Dumfries, Lawrence went through his old court papers to find his ex-wife Bernice's phone number. He only found Liz and Andrew's home phone number; he used to call collect from the Onslow Prison. He hesitated to call his ex-family-in-law because of their negative view of him. Anke encouraged him to call to get his ex-wife's phone number, who definitively knew his children's whereabouts. Finally, Lawrence called the Dove's residence phone number, and Liz picked up the phone to be surprised it was Lawrence Jackson. She was shocked that Lawrence didn't call collect and use a personal cell phone. She asked Lawrence why he didn't call collect at this time. She became upset when Lawrence clearly stated the reason for his call to get Bernice's phone number and take custody of his children. Before Liz would give up Bernice's phone number, she lectured Lawrence on how happy her daughter was with her new husband and wouldn't accept any interference. Lawrence had to promise not to interfere in Bernice's relationship with Leonardo James three times before Liz gave him the phone number. Anke was there to chop down the phone number Lawrence called out loud and clearly on a piece of paper. Anke dialed the number and handed the phone to her husband, who was still thinking about what he should say and what he shouldn't say:

"Hello," a female voice answered the phone, which Lawrence recognized.

"Good evening, Bernice. How are you doing?"

"Fine, and thanks. Who's calling?".

"This is Lawrence. Lawrence Jackson". There was a moment of silence where Bernice tried to process the person on the phone.

"Where you're calling from?".

"I'm calling from Virginia. I want to come and see my two kids".

"Joshua and Grace are with their grandparents."

"Make arrangements for me to see them next Saturday."

"Ok. I'll let my mother know you're coming Saturday to see them". Bernice hung up while her new husband stood behind, trying to figure out who was on the phone and what the call was about. On the other hand, Lawrence and Anke hugged each other in a jubilee dance of victory, singing:" We're going to Georgia. We're going to Georgia." They were thrilled. They sang and danced all night, hoping to finally meet Joshua and Grace after these years of separation. Many questions around the wellbeing of kids' conditions with their grandparents aroused the determination of Anke and Lawrence to see the children: were they well-fed or malnourished? Lawrence resumed his job after meeting with Mr. Richardson to go over the outcome of his mission to the United Kingdom. Anke would visit the construction site in Arlington every week to monitor the Paramount Construction Company's progress. She wanted the company to finish the two hundred units of buildings promptly so she could launch the phase of attracting new tenants. For that matter, Anke had contact with the Southern Management Company, which already had many properties throughout Virginia. Anke was going to hand the management of her building to the well-known Southern Management Company while she would oversee the financial aspects of the business. Anke booked a room at the Renaissance Concourse in College Park, Georgia, close to the Hartsfield-Jackson International Airport of Atlanta. She also purchased two Southwest plane tickets online for two hours round flight from Virginia to Georgia. The trip to Georgia emblazed a lot of excitement and fulfillment in Lawrence's house. It was considered a great accomplishment and a sense of being whole. Anke couldn't wait to see Lawrence's children for the first time and meet his ex-wife, Bernice whom she heard a lot about. Many thoughts were going through her mind that she didn't want to discuss with her husband. She didn't know if these people were going to accept her because of her origin or because of her skin color. She became very anxious and, at the same time, delighted about the occasion. Her mixed-matched feeling grew more prominent as the day approached. Emotionally unbalanced, Anke tried hard to overcome the feeling of possible rejection and denigration that intermittently was coming over her. The night before they took the Southwest Airlines flight to Atlanta, Georgia, Lawrence called Bernice to confirm the time of his visit. He was instructed to meet his children at their grandparents' house in Cobb County at eleven o'clock in the morning. On the day of the flight, Anke woke up early to pack Lawrence's suitcase with his expensive clothes. She parked all her nice outfits in her favorite pink Louis Vuitton duffle bag and put on her expensive jewelry. Lawrence walked to the Hertz Car Rental counter when the flight landed at the Hartsfield-Jackson International Airport. He rented a white Cadillac Escalade and drove his wife to the Renaissance Concourse in College Park, five minutes from the airport. They had a spacious room with a king-size bed in the hotel, giving them a beautiful overview of the city of Atlanta. After checking-in in at the hotel, Lawrence and Anke put on their best outfits and hopped on the white Cadillac Escalade in the direction of Cobb County. Lawrence rang the bell of the Dove's residence, and Andrew came out to open the door and greeted the couple in a relaxed manner. Lawrence sensed trouble in the air before entering the Dove's living room, holding Anke's left hand. The Dove's living room scenery wasn't conducive to a peaceful gathering. It was like a meeting of two antagonist teams about to start a fierce battle. The two children sat on the living room couch, sandwiched between Liz and Andrew. Their mother was sitting on a separate chair beside her father, holding her new baby in her arms. Anke and Lawrence were given the loveseat facing the opposition team, where no one was smiling or talking. The two kids refused any eye contact with their father, who tried unsuccessfully twice to shake their hands. They had their head down and weren't answering any questions from the visitors as instructed. Finally, Liz broke the silence after everyone was aware of the antipathic atmosphere in the house.

"What's the reason for your visit?" Liz opened the discussion.

"First, allow me to present to you my wife, Anke. We're here to ask my two kids to come and live with us in Virginia, where we have a big house" Lawrence went straight to the issue.

"Over my dead body. I spend money caring for your kids for five years. Now, you come to take them away. It's going to be a long legal battle, and I'm ready for it," Liz said, with anger raging out of her voice.

"How much do you think you've spent on my kids?" questioned Lawrence.

"About twenty thousand dollars now," affirmed Liz looking at her husband Andrew nodding.

"We're here to work things out for the good of these two children," continued Lawrence. Before he even finished his sentence, Anke reached out of her pink purse, a checkbook, and wrote a check for twenty thousand dollars that she handed Liz. Liz was shocked, with her mouth wide open. Andrew was in a state of unbelief, squeezing Bernice whose eyes were clicking uncontrollably for a long period of time.

"Here're your children. They're yours" Liz stood up holding the check in her right hand, and the meeting was over. Before the gathering ended, Lawrence gave specific instructions for returning the children. Joshua and Grace would spend a day in the Renaissance Concourse Hotel with Lawrence and Anke. Since they were still in school, Lawrence would buy a plane ticket for them to spend each weekend in Virginia until school would be over. The smooth transition would help the children adjust to their new family and home in a different environment. Lawrence took his two children to the Lenox Square Mall in Atlanta without any objection from the grandparents or from the mother. Lawrence and Anke purchased beautiful and costly outfits for the children and bought each of them an iPhone.

Lawrence called his phone service provider in the mall to add two lines for his children. Joshua and Grace were inundated with joy, jumping and hugging their parents, who rejoiced to see them display their personalities. Anke reassured them to call whenever they had a problem with anybody, whether at home or school. The children's confidence returned, knowing they could trust their father and stepmother. They went to the Lenox Square Mall's food court to eat different food from various cultures. There was Chinese cuisine, Japanese cuisine, Italian cuisine, Moroccan cuisine, and much more than the kids could taste. It was the kids' first experience eating out since they lived with their grandparents, who never left their comfort zone. After eating, the two children started to voice the mistreatments they underwent in their grandparents' house. Lawrence drove the entire family to the hotel to spend time together. They went to the hotel swimming pool to start teaching the kids how to swim because there was a swimming pool awaiting them in Virginia. As night fell, Lawrence decided to take the children back, but they cried, refused to go back, and wanted to spend the night with Lawrence. The following day he took them back before he dropped the rental car at the Hertz and boarded the Southwest Aircraft with Anke to Virginia.

Chapter 20

The Jacksons acquiring properties in Virginia

The following Friday, right after school, Liz and Andrew dropped Joshua and Grace at the Atlanta airport to fly to Dulles Airport to visit their father. Liz provided them with a duffle bag containing their respective clothes and the school backpack for the trip. The flight was about two hours, and the aircraft landed at the Dulles International Airport at five o'clock. From the plane on the ground, Joshua and Grace called their father, who was waiting by Anke's side for them in the airport hall. The children entered the airport hall and joyfully jumped into their father's and stepmother's arms. Grace clung to Anke, unwilling to let her go because of a special bond already weaved between the two at their first meeting. Lawrence put them all in his silver Nissan Murano and drove to their new house in Dumfries. The house was magnificent, and the children couldn't believe their eyes. The house had a metallic fence around it with different flowers and trees. A giant iron gate led into the front yard of the house. There was a seven hundred feet drive from the massive entrance to the double-car garage on the right side of the house. The same remote control that opened the iron gate also opened the garage door. There was a door from the garage that led into a large living room which was covered entirely with a beautiful sky-blue tick carpet. In the middle of the living room was brand-new golden genius leather furniture. There was a golden fireplace in the wall facing the furniture. On top of the fireplace was a gigantic thin-screen TV well framed in the wall. From the living room, people could see the beautiful and fully equipped kitchen, which floor was covered with white transparent ceramic tiles. The kitchen had a big double doors refrigerator full of food and a chest freezer full of frozen food and meat. The dining room was adjacent to the kitchen, featuring a long prodigy table surrounded by ten royal chairs. The lower level of the house had two rooms and a full bathroom. The first room was turned into an office with many office equipment like a computer, printer, fax machine, Xerox machine, desk, chair, and more. This room also had a WiFi system that allowed internet connection throughout the house. The second room was reserved for guests who might visit the family and stay for a few days. In the back of the living room was a stairway that mounted up to the upper floor of the house. The upper level was also covered with the same tick blue carpet, soft like a feather and pretty like the sky. The upper floor had three rooms and two bathrooms, one in the master room where Lawrence and Anke slept. The two rooms belonged to Joshua and Grace and were equipped identically except for the color of the bedsheets and pillows. The children's rooms had one bunk bed, a chair next to a table, an apple computer, a tablet, and a 38" TV on the wall. The upper-level bathroom was between the children's rooms and the master. To the far left of the house while entering was a swimming pool surrounded by light. The colorful light inside the swimming pool gave a gorgeous view of the front yard at night. When the children considered everything in their rooms and the state of unbelief they were in, they went to Lawrence, sitting in the living room with Anke, and asked:

"Dad! Is this your house?".

"Yes. This is our house". Joshua and Grace started jumping joyfully, hugging and kissing their father and stepmother, laughing hysterically. The children had an unforgettable time with their father: they ate, cooked their own food, watched their TV show, and learned how to swim. They didn't want to return to Georgia, yet they boarded the plane back to Atlanta with bitter tears in their eyes.

Meanwhile, the Australian Prime Minister called the White House to request an assistance from the FBI for the murder of a famous tennis player in Sydney. The tennis player's house was on the outskirts of the city of Sydney where he was gun downed. There were many trees in front of the house which was locked down for a thoroughly investigation. The Prime Minister insisted that a Cork Theory FBI agent could help crack the case. Mr. Max Richardson submitted the demand to Lawrence who appointed one of his assistants, Keith Ross, to travel to Australia after gathering all the essential equipment for the job. Lawrence didn't want to take on the assignment, because the construction of his apartment building was in full swing.

The Paramount Construction Company completed the apartment building in Arlington, Virginia, in less than a year. At no time the Southern Management Company filled the building with tenants. All the rent should come between the first and fifth of each month, and any late payment had a five percent late charge added according to the lease agreement. Between the tenth and fifteenth of the month, Anke personally visited the building to handle the business's accounting. She would send half of the collected rent to the Wells Fargo Bank for mortgage payment and the insurance policy on the property. She would also pay Southern Management Company money for managing the business and put some money into the equipment amortization account. Every month, the Jackson property would make a net profit of $50,000, which would be transferred to the couple's bank account. Within six months, the Jacksons realized the business was very lucrative and returned to the Wells Fargo Bank loan officer to duplicate their business model in Alexandria, Virginia. Lawrence and Anke agreed to give the bank the ownership paper of the Arlington Building as collateral to secure another eight million dollars. Less than a year, the Paramount Construction Company finish a new apartment building for the Jacksons in Alexandria. Lawrence and Anke made a net profit of $50,000 monthly from the new building, which was also transferred to their bank account. In about six months in the business, the Jackson family became smutty rich and didn't know what to do with the money coming in.

On the other hand, Lawrence was doing very well in investigating crimes committed in all fifty States of America. In every state he visited, he managed to convict one or two criminals who escaped justice. Major news outlets like Los Angeles Times and New York Times were following his work and giving updated information about the prison term of the criminals after conviction in court. The situation caused criminals in every city in America to turn against the Tree Cork Detective. People who knew they had committed an unsolved crime followed him and tried to chase him out of their city. Lawrence found his life in danger anywhere he went to collect evidence against criminals. He was pursued by criminals looking to run him over or attack him physically while on duty.

An incident in Chicago, Illinois, made him rethink the practice of his duty and not be involved personally in the incarceration of criminals. Two men were pursuing him on the street of Chicago and police had to intervene to take him to a crime site where he was supposed to collect a tree cork. After the incident, Lawrence met with FBI director Max Richardson to redefine his job description and performance. The meeting concluded that Lawrence would start training FBI agents on the Tree Cork Theory in his unit at Quantico Lab. Mr. Richardson decided to make all FBI agents take a class on the seventh floor of the FBI crime laboratory in Quantico, Virginia, on how the Tree Cork Theory worked. All FBI field operators from all fifty states would know how to collect images from tree cork and to know whom to target in their investigations. Lawrence didn't travel anymore for his job but spent more time engaging his children and wife in extracurricular activities and church work.

A Sunday morning service in the Dumfries Baptist Church brought a tone of guilt over Lawrence for the hurts he had caused others in his past. He was sad all all-day, dragging heavy remorse on his heart, and he couldn't sleep. First, he tried to hide his filling from his wife who was constantly asking to know what was wrong. The more he refused to admit his problem, the more miserable he became at home and work. Finally, Lawrence called his wife Anke to their master room and narrated all the crimes he had committed and his time in prison. In addition, he decided to pay a restitution to the closest family members of his victims in College Park, Georgia. Anke was shocked to know the filthy past of her husband but was determined to back him up through the restitution phase of his life. The two decided to return to College Park and look for Mr. Gerald Menefee, who might still live in his old apartment. The following Saturday, they flew to Atlanta and knocked on Mr. Gerald's apartment door. Gerald Menefee opened the door and asked his potential visitors whom they were looking for because he couldn't recognize Lawrence Jackson. With some hesitation, he let them into his apartment and wanted to know why they were visiting. Lawrence explained that their visit was to inquire about his life after his wife's death and to find out how he could help. Living on a fixed retirement income, Gerald had difficulty paying rent and a car note his wife left behind. After the conversation, Lawrence and Anke promised Gerald to purchase him a new house in a quiet neighborhood of Jonesboro, Georgia. Besides, they promised to pay off the Tesla X model electric car Mrs. Menefee left behind. The same day, Lawrence and Anke took Gerald to Jonesboro for house hunting and found a Realtor Agent. Lawrence and Anke paid $120,000 for the house Gerald chose in Jonesboro and went on Tesla's website to pay $30,000 to clean the car note on the electric car. They flew back to Virginia very happy about their accomplishment but faced the challenge of finding Brendon Lyle, Michelle Cornett's only son. It took them two weeks to finally contact Brendon Lyle, who worked in a mechanic garage in Newark, New Jersey. Lawrence and Anke had a long phone conversation to determine the issue Brendon faced to know how they could help. After high school, Brendon wanted to attend cyber security training but couldn't because of a lack of financial resources. Lawrence Anke paid $70,000 for a six-month internship and certification in a state-accredited institution in Newark. After the certification, Brendon got a cyber security job at the Jersey Water Company based in Newark, New Jersey.

Chapter 21

The first visit

Lawrence's children's first visit was a poignant and surprising experience. Josh, a sixth-grader, and Grace, a fifth-grader, were still in the tender years of their childhood. Before the children stirred from their sleep on a Saturday morning, Lawrence had arranged for their tutors to be present. Mr. Crosby, Josh's private tutor, and Ms. Rebecca Hudson, Grace's tutor, were waiting in Jackson's residence, ready to meet the children as they woke up around 9:00 a.m. after their morning routine. Mr. Crosby was an old-age middle school teacher from Fairfax County Public Schools District. Anke offered them a delicious morning breakfast in the dining room, where Lawrence introduced the children to their respective dedicated private instructors. The tutors' role was not just to follow the children's educational progress and supply them with additional learning material but to constantly contact them for their academic success. Their unwavering dedication and commitment to the children's progress was evident in their daily chats with the students after school to determine their academic progress in Georgia. This dedication was a testament to Lawrence's belief in the value of education. Ms. Rebecca and Grace bonded immediately, and their connection was a source of comfort and reassurance. Grace took her to her room to show her schoolbook bag, a sign of the trust and warmth in their relationship. It was clear that the little girl had been waiting for someone to help her with her school difficulties. Since she separated from her father, Grace had been struggling with school and learning. Ms. Rebecca reassured the little girl that she would guide her successfully through her school challenges. The two embraced one another, their bond a source of comfort and reassurance, and wouldn't let go when Lawrence's loud voice sounded throughout the whole house:

"It's time to go. We have a long day ahead of us," Lawrence's voice echoed through the house, breaking the tender moment. Brimming with excitement for the day's adventures, the children were eager to start their exploration journey. They bid their tutors farewell and hopped into their father's car, ready for the day's surprises. In the trunk of the silver Nissan Murano, Anke had placed a big white cooler containing different types of ice creams and goodies for the event. They set off on a 2h30 drive to the Virginia Zoo, where Lawrence had already purchased the tickets for the whole family online. When they parked their vehicle, they realized the parking lot was almost complete because of the number of people visiting the zoo on weekends. The admission into the zoo was swift and easy without any complications. The entrance was a massive, lovely building with green roofing, giving the impression of a modern train station. It was a 53-acre animal Inhabitant adjacent to Lafayette Park in Norfolk, Virginia. There were different sections in the zoo with a little over 700 animals. Each section had its unique animals according to their origin. Some animals were from Asia, Africa,

Madagascar, North America, and South America. Every section of the zoo had a peculiar name that characterized the animals that lived there.

The Jacksons chose to visit the Trail of the Tiger, an Asian group of animals like tigers, orangutans, binturongs, red pandas, and rhinoceros hornbills. Josh and Grace, their eyes wide with wonder, had the opportunity to interact with some of the animals. They gave bananas to some orangutans, who smiled at them as a gesture of thanks and appreciation. Then, the Jacksons went to the Okavango Delta, which exhibited African animals. They could admire some giraffes, zebras, lions, cheetahs, meerkats, elephants, gazelles, and giant tortoises over 200 years old. In the third section they visited, they could contemplate Northern America animals like bison, prairie dogs, pumas, and bald eagles. Josh and Grace had the opportunity to get up close and personal with some animals they could feed with bananas and oranges. The children's faces lit up with excitement as they fed the animals, their wonder at the experience evident. Lawrence's children were so amazed by the knowledge that they came out of the zoo speechless, their minds buzzing with new information and experiences. They all realized they were hungry when they got into their Murano to leave. They all got tired from walking from place to place in the zoo, but they couldn't feel it because of the excitement in the zoo. Anke took from a container of cheeseburgers and milkshakes she had prepared for the occasion. They all ate and drank the milkshakes as if they had not eaten for days. They spent about twenty minutes enjoying the burgers and the milkshakes before heading to their next destination. They drove to the Virginia Beach Aquarium south of Rudee Inlet for thirty minutes. The aquarium was divided into three sections, namely, the North Building, the South Building, and the Nature Trail. The aquarium was massive, holding 800,00 gallons of fresh and saltwater. It contained 700 different species. The aquarium was all glass with a tunnel where people could walk through and admire various fish moving freely above the visitors. Walking through the aquarium made Lawrence's children so close to the fish. The harmony between different kinds of fish thriving peacefully in the same environment was striking. All the fish in the tank were different colors and shapes, swimming freely. Josh and Grace, their eyes sparkling with pure joy, were learning and growing from the educational value of the aquarium experience. Their faces lit up with every new fish they discovered, and their laughter filled the air, adding to the lively atmosphere of the aquarium.

The Jackson family left the aquarium, heading to Virginia Beach, with many "Wow" on the children's lips. They got to the beach around 5:00 p.m. Dimmed in the sky, the sun rays were pleasant, and a slightly cool breeze was whistling and brushing their faces. Lawrence took the white cooler from the vehicle's trunk, and Anke grabbed a large blanket she had stored in the back of the car. They walked to the ever-ending beach and the fantastic crystal sands. Anke spread the large green blanket for all of them to see on and contemplate the waves and the sea, which gave the impression of touching the sky in the distance.

Meanwhile, Lawrence retrieved some ice cream corn and crackers from the cooler and distributed them to each other. The children, their eyes wide with wonder, were reticent to eat their ice cream and crackers, overwhelmed by the beauty of nature. There were people on the beach as far as the eye could see. Some were walking and talking. Others sat under colorful umbrellas to savor the moment. The unforgettable experience of the day created a breakable bond between parents and children. Josh leaned his head against his father while Anke held Grace tightly on her lap. The Jacksons enjoyed each other's company without realizing that the time was flying by. When they discovered the darkness covering the beach, Anke's watch displayed 6:15 p.m., and they had to drive 2h30 back home.

Anke and Lawrence decided to have dinner in a nearby hotel because the children would have fallen asleep when they reached Dumfries. Right behind where they were sitting was the Embassy Suite by Hilton. Anke and Lawrence wrapped up the cooler and the green blanket and went to the Embassy Suites lobby, where they could see the sign of the hotel restaurant. As soon as they sat down, a waitress came to them and handed them the menu book. The waitress approached them as if she knew them before or if she knew that they were from far away. They ordered different food from the menu, and their plates were set before them. The restaurant was big and very friendly, with chairs well organized around beautiful tables. Classical music was playing in the background. The food was very delicious, and the service was delightful. They could see the darkness out waiting for them from the restaurant windows.

Lawrence suggested they have a room in the hotel and drive home the next day. But Anke objected vigorously to Lawrence's proposal because she didn't want the children to miss the Sunday service at the Dumfries Baptist Church. With full bellies, the Jacksons left with an impressive tip for the waitress and hopped on their silver Murano. Before they could reach Dumfries, the children singing in the vehicle were asleep in the back seat. They arrived home around 9:30 p.m. and exhausted and went straight to bed, leaving everything they took with them in the vehicle. They all slept until Anke was the first to wake up and prepare breakfast for the family. After breakfast, she woke the rest of the family members to shower and prepare for church.

The children couldn't stop expressing their gratitude to their parents at the breakfast table, their words filled with love and appreciation for the beautiful day they had. At church, Josh and Grace went into the Sunday School classes of their respective age. Before the service was over, they made a lot of friends. Sunday School was nothing new to them. They had memorized a lot of bible stories while in the care of their grandparents, Liz and Andrew. They could interact with children of their age and get to know them. Josh made more friends and exchanged his phone number with many kids, including the pastor's son. They both clicked together as twins belonging to the same age group. Pastor Carlos Montpelier, the pastor of the Dumfries Baptist Church, had two children: Mark, who was 11 years old, and Sheila, who was 9. At the end of the Sunday service, pastor Carlos invited the Jackson family for lunch at his house because Anke informed them that Lawrence's children were coming for a visit.

Pastor Carlos, his wife Cydny, and their two children lived ten minutes from the church. After the church service, the Jacksons responded to the pastor's invitation. Carlos and his family lived in a big house with a large dining room with a long, well-decorated table in the center. The table was extendable and could comfortably accommodate twelve people. Cydny had prepared some delicious dishes from

Italian cuisine. There were different kinds of pasta and pizzas on the table. There are many different sodas, some on the table, some in a cooler, and others in a large refrigerator in the kitchen. Before they all started eating, pastor Carlos presented his family members, and Lawrence did the same.

The two families ate and drank together to get to know each other better. When Carlos learned that Lawrence worked for the FBI, his eyes lit up to know more about his duties. But Lawrence wouldn't briefly detail his responsibilities at the FBI forensics laboratory in Quantico, Virginia. When the adults were having their moment to know one another, Marc took Josh by the hands down into the basement of the house. The two young girls followed them down. The basement was huge and well organized, with different games for children. There was table tennis, pool table, Nintendo, Scribe, puzzles, domino, chess, and checker. The two boys started playing table tennis while the girls were playing domino. After some moments of table tennis, the boys went on the chess board, which Josh knew nothing about. Mark was happy to show Josh how to play chess. It consisted of sixteen black pieces, again sixteen white pieces. Each team had one king, one queen, two rooks, two bishops, two knights, and eight pawns.

Josh assimilated the chess so quickly that the two were into the game without knowing the time was flying. It was about 3:00 p.m. when the adults came down to separate the kids because Josh and Grace had to be at the airport by 4 o'clock. The children wouldn't separate from one another if Lawrence didn't stand his ground. He drove his children home to get their bookbags and clothes and headed to the Dulles International Airport. Josh and Grace were supposed to be at the airport by 4:00 p.m. to catch their flight back to Atlanta. When they became conscious of their return to Georgia, Josh, and Grace started weeping deeply and begging their father and stepmother to save them from the misery they lived in back home. They were crying at the airport, where their father managed to get them on a Southwest flight. They cried in the aircraft until they landed at the Hartsfield-Jackson Atlanta Airport, where their mother and grandmother were waiting impatiently for them. When Bernice and Liz picked up Josh and Grace at the airport, they were still crying and couldn't tell why. It took them a couple of days to open up about all they had experienced in Virginia. The parental love and affection they received from Lawrence and Anke were immemorable to their souls, and they had no words to express them.

Chapter 22

Inmate returning to Los Angeles

After his prison term, Jason Sullivan was dropped off at a bus stop that could take him to Charlotte. He had a plastic bag containing a few clothes, the release papers, and four hundred dollars from working in the prison. After two hours, he was sitting at the bus stop when the Bus 550, the direction Charlotte engraved on the front, came in. Jason went to the bus driver for instructions on getting to the Charlotte Greyhound Bus Station. The trip was long, dragging with many stops and changing three buses to reach the Greyhound Bus Station. Jason was hungry, but his determination overpowered his entire being so that all his eyes were in Los Angeles, the city he grew up in.

Jason Sullivan reached Charlotte Greyhound Bus Station around 4:00 p.m. to learn that all the buses to Los Angeles were already full. The next available seat was on a bus leaving Charlotte at 11:55 p.m., and it would take two days to reach Los Angeles. Jason purchased the bus fare for $170.99 and went to find a seat in the corner of the bus station sitting hall. He left the plastic bag containing his clothes on the seat to secure the spot and went to the vending machines on the other side of the sitting hall. Jason got a couple of bags of chips and a soda, then walked back to his seat. Many people were in the hall, but he failed to identify any of them. Jason Sullivan wanted to find someone to talk to, but after eating the chips and drinking the soda, Jason fell asleep on the seat, his plastic bag on his lap. The loud noises in the sitting hall didn't bother him, and he slept for four hours. After he woke up around 8 o'clock, the darkness overshadowed the bus station, and the lights in the sitting hall were sending clarity. Jason realized the plastic bag had fallen and his discharge prison papers were on the floor. He quickly picked up the documents and put them in the plastic bag with his clothes. Jason didn't want people to know he was an inmate from the Onslow Prison boarding a Greyhound bus with them. Jason Sullivan felt the need to use the bathroom at the end of the sitting hall but didn't know how to hold his seat. He checked the ticket in his pocket and proceeded to the restroom area. After urinating, he washed his hands when he saw his face in the mirror above the faucets. Jason didn't like what he saw. His face was dry, with two identical lines between his nose and cheeks. His cheeks were saggy, and his lips were dry and chipping. Seventeen years in prison have affected his appearance, making him look older than his years. Tears started to come down his cheeks, but he wiped them off, saying, "I have my brighter days ahead of me."

The speakers in the sitting hall announced that the boarding process to Los Angeles began around 11:30 p.m. Jason got in line at the door of a long green Greyhound Bus with his bus ticket in his right hand and his bag in his left hand. Standing at the bus entrance, the bus driver checked each passenger's ticket to ensure they all had the correct destination pass. Jason

Sullivan sat comfortably at the very rear of the bus and put his plastic bag underneath his seat. The two-day trip was like an eternity for him. Every three hours of drive, the chauffeur would stop at a McDonell or Burger King for the passengers to stretch their legs and purchase something to eat. Jason's mind was focused on one thing-finding the hidden money. He hated these unnecessary stops, which made the trip drag and time-consuming. Sometimes, he refused to get off the bus to stretch his feet or get something to eat. He wanted to use only some money on the trip, knowing he would need transportation to get to his booty. After two days of agonizing trip, the Greyhound Bus made it safe and sound to the Downtown Los Angeles bus station at 1:40 a.m. when all activities in the city died down. People were getting off the bus and jumping into the arms of their relatives, waiting for them. Some other passengers were calling UBER to take them home. Jason was the only passenger left in the bus parking lot. All the people he traveled with left him stranded. He checked his pocket to realize he had only $70. Jason Sullivan wanted to walk to where he had hidden the money. But he refused that advice because Los Angeles was a dangerous city at night. He decided to sleep at the Greyhound Bus Station until morning before going to look for his hidden treasure. Jason laid down on a bus station bench and used the plastic bag containing his clothes as a pillow. He tried to sleep, but the sleep wasn't coming. He closed his eyes hard, but sleep wasn't coming.

The images of violence in the Onslow Prison were passing through his face. Jason was living the high and the low moments of his life in prison. Tears were coming down his cheeks uncontrollably, and a distinctive smile was at the corner of his lips. The smile on his face was the sign of victory and the financial freedom he longed for. Jason started laughing hysterically when the image of the black leather bag containing the $400,000 ATM money passed by his face. He was still contemplating the black leather bag when he fell asleep. Jason woke up around 8:00 a.m. when the sun sent some piercing rays to Jason's face. He woke up asking people for a bus that could take him down Hoover Street. Finally, Jason spoke to a UBER driver who just dropped a rider and was willing to take Jason to his spot for $20. Jason knew it was a rape-off, but he didn't have time to argue. The UBER driver collected the $20 before opening the car door for Jason. When the driver dropped Jason at the corner of Hoover Street and W. Vernon Avenue, he couldn't believe the area's transformation. New businesses and the cleanness of the area struck him. A new white house was on the vacant lot where Jason Sullivan buried the black leather bag containing the ATM money. At first, Jason thought the UBER driver made a mistake and dropped him somewhere strange. He walked around the block twice to ensure he was at the proper location. At that realization, he started trembling and shaking from inside. Jason went to the white house on his childhood vacant lot and rang the bell with his hands shaking violently. A middle-aged Asian lady answered the door. She crack-opened the door to see the face of the person ringing the doorbell.

- "What can I do for you?" she asked in a broken English.
- "Did you see ...?" Answered Jason, pointing at where he had buried the money.
- "Did you see what?" The Asian lady asked calmly.

- "Yes, did you see...?" Jason repeated, pointing at the spot where he had hidden the money with a trembling voice and red eyes.
- "I said, did you what?" With an angry voice, the Asian lady commanded him.

At that time, Jason's mind went blank, and his mouth was wide open. He couldn't let any sounds out, and his finger still pointed at the spot where the money had been hidden.

- "Who is that, honey?" The husband of the Asian lady asked from inside the house.
- "It is a madman at the door". The woman responded to her husband.
- "What does the madman want?" The voice from inside asked.
- "I don't know what the madman is saying" . The lady turned to her husband after slamming the door in Jason's face.

Jason Sullivan became a madman in the streets of Los Angeles, pushing a shopping cart containing his few clothes and the prison release documents.

Miguel was an immigrant from El Salvador. His father was a farmer who owned 10 acres of land in San Vicente, El Salvador. However, due to a lack of financial resources, Mr. Escabar could only farm up to 4 acres to feed his family. He vowed to do everything in his power to send his first child, Miguel, through a higher education so that he could take over one day. But deep down in his heart, he didn't want to be a farmer, seeing the toiling of his parents. Miguel loved to go to school and was among the brilliant students in his class. He was the sunshine of his family. Miguel had a younger sister who also loved to go to school. She couldn't go far in education because the family didn't believe in women's education. Miguel was in San Vicente Grande High School when his father tragically passed away from a pneumonia complication. The sickness didn't take long before taking away Mr. Escabar, the family's central piece and sole breadwinner.

Should this tragic event deter Miguel from going to school? Mrs. Maria Escobar took over the farm and started producing maize and cassava to feed her two kids, ensuring that Miguel continued his education. Maria believed Miguel would follow in his father's footsteps and embrace agriculture. At the University of San Salvador, Miguel studied Central American Literature to become a school- teacher, a promising career in the country. Miguel would stay with one of his uncles in San Salvador to go to school and return to his mother in San Vicente on weekends. After completing his four years of college, Miguel applied for teaching jobs in all the educational institutions in El Salvador. His applications were consistently rejected for minor reasons. Sometimes, there was a lack of experience or too many applicants, and the government couldn't satisfy all the demands. Miguel lost hope and became obnoxious for continuing to burden his mother. His mother always comforted him, saying that one day, the door to a good job would open for him.

One day, Miguel was helping her mother plant cassava when he heard about another Central American caravan heading to the United States. He said to himself, "The occasion wouldn't bypass him this time." Miguel took his college diplomas, passport, identification card, and clothes and joined the caravan. His mother objected to the decision, but Miguel convinced his mother that he would get a teaching position in America and earn good money to support his mother. Through his Facebook and WhatsApp accounts, he traced the site of the caravan formation to the city of San Pedro Sula in Honduras. Miguel quickly traveled to Honduras to take part in the final instructions for the risky journey. By the time he got to San Pedro Sula, the number of participants in the caravan had increased to 2,500. A sense of brotherhood embraced all the participants after the final instructions, which consisted of caring for one another and everyone's duty to look after the children and the weak. People in the caravan were eager to share their food and their knowledge of what to expect from US immigration officials.

The journey took over three months to reach the city of Tijuana, where migrants gathered in a camp for processing one by one and case by case. Miguel spent about two weeks in the processing center before being allowed to enter the US. He gave one of his mother's relative's address in Long Beach, California. Miguel took a Greyhound Bus from San Diogo to Long Beach and called his uncle Felipe Hernandez. Miguel had to spend the afternoon at the Greyhound station until Felipe got off work and picked him up. When Miguel got into Felipe's one-bedroom apartment, he saw some women cooking and a lot of children watching TV. Miguel asked himself why there were so many people in a single apartment.

Felipe had to introduce him to all the families sharing the same apartment and explain the living conditions. Felipe and his family shared their one-bedroom apartment with two other families. The men in the apartment shared equitably the rent, which was $2,000, and the women provided for food, and the children were charged to everyone. With vibrant faces, three ladies in the kitchen were preparing evening dinner for everybody. The rules in the apartment were straightforward. All the men chipped in at the end of every month to pay the rent, and the women's responsibilities were to buy and prepare food for everyone regardless of origin and status. The women worked in the same grocery store, Arteaga Market, and purchased half-price groceries.

The three men in the apartment worked for the same construction company, Trojans Construction Inc., that received contracts in all of Los Angeles and beyond. In the morning, from Monday through Friday, the men woke up at 5:00 a.m. to shower until 6:00 a.m. when they would leave for work. Felipe owned an old Ford F250 with an extra cab and a long bed full of different work tools. They used the pickup truck to go to work and purchase meat and drinks on weekends. At 7:00 a.m., the kids would wake up, shower, and dress for school. One of the women would take the children to the bus stop, just at the apartment complex's entrance. The school provided breakfast for the children in the morning and lunch at 11:00. After the children had gone to school, the women would take turns to shower and prepare a breakfast for themselves. At 9:00 a.m., the women would drive to work, and a peaceful silence resounded in the apartment until evening. The three women put together money to purchase a Toyota Camry, which they utilized to go to work and visit family and friends on weekends. At 2:30 p.m., one of the wives would ask permission from work to come home and get the children from the bus stop. The women rotated every week to ensure that the children shouldn't be home by themselves since they weren't 13 yet. The designated woman would stay with the children until all adults returned home.

Felipe, his wife, and his three children slept in the only room of the apartment. The remaining occupants shared the living room, divided into two sections before Miguel's arrival.

With his arrival, Miguel would occupy the dining area. At night, before sleeping, the furniture in the apartment was to be reorganized to yield more room. The couch turned upside down, and the central table and the loveseat were on top. The blue blanket occupying the first section belonged to Mr. Castillo, his wife, and his two daughters. The purple blanket covering the second section belonged to Mr. Lopez, his wife, and his two sons. The red blanket belonged to Miguel and would occupy the dining area after the dining chairs were laid on the table. Between the living room and the single room of the apartment was a little closet divided into three parts for the three families. Saturdays, no one worked, and they were considered days of jubilation with loud music and booze. Miguel was home for two weeks before the Trojans Construction Company agreed to hire him. Since he had no construction skills, he was paid $400 a week and had to contribute $500 for rent each month and some gas money occasionally.

Miguel's asylum application was denied within three months, and a thirty-day window was open for him to file an appeal. The men and women in his household discouraged him from getting into legal complications. He should be content with working a construction job and making some money every week. Miguel didn't want to be in construction, but he couldn't tell his hosts, who immensely enjoyed their careers and lifestyles. Miguel hated the construction job but had no other options.

A typical Saturday in the apartment was a day of rejoicing from construction work. Loud Mexican music was played all day, barbeques were grilled, and liquor was available for all adults. Sunday morning was a time to recuperate from Saturday extravagances. Sunday afternoon, Miguel and his hosts joined other Latinos and Latinas from all corners of Long Beach to meet in the city park for games. The gathering in the park was a precious time of socialization among the Latinos, a time to make friends and learn about situations in Central America. Miguel didn't like the construction work and wanted to become a schoolteacher. He talked to many people coming out to Sunday afternoon socialization to see if anyone could help him become a schoolteacher in California. No matter who Miguel entertained with his dream, the answer remained: "Your goal was too high for an undocumented non-English speaker. You better be content with your construction job".

After three years of construction work, Miguel became tired of his lifestyle and the lifestyle of those around him. Miguel learned that learning English well was the first step toward his goal. English was the only way he could communicate his knowledge to his students. He received information about an English class held weekly in a church from 6:00 p.m. to 8:00 p.m., Monday through Friday. Miguel enrolled and started the class to find out that one of his classmates, Rosa, lived in a house adjacent to his apartment complex. After his construction work, Miguel would ride with his new friend Rose to class and back home safely. After three years in construction, he had enough and wanted instead to devote all his time to the English language. Miguel was in a big dilemma. How would he pay his share of the rent if he quit the construction job? He would be kicked out of the apartment and lose his privilege of food and drink. In the middle of his dilemma, the Trojans Construction company signed a new contract to build a new house south of Downtown Los Angeles. One early Monday morning, Miguel and his team started to clear brushes on a vacant lot at the corner of South Hoover Street and West Vernon Avenue to build a new house.

Miguel was clearing the bush along the cement fence of the vacant lot while the other crew members were demolishing the woody structure on the lot. Miguel stumbled on a shallow hole with a black leather bag containing money. He pulled the bag out and turned his back to call his team members to witness the findings. But his crew members needed help in their demolishing activities. Miguel covered the black leather bag with plastic and hid it among the construction tools in the trunk of Felipe's Ford F250 pickup truck. Miguel debated whether it would be wise to tell his hosts or keep all to himself for the whole day. At the end of the working day, when the crew made it home, Miguel took the black leader bag wrapped up in plastic to his closet. He announced to his hosts that he wouldn't work the next day. The following day, Miguel woke up early, as usual, to watch people in the apartment go about their morning routines. The women were the last to leave with their Toyota Camry at 9:00 a.m. for the Orteaga Mexican supermarket. Miguel reorganized the furniture in the apartment and put every piece back in their normal position. He locked the apartment door and went straight to the closet to pull out the black leather bag. He put the bag on the dining table and opened it to assess the value of the money. Miguel was shocked to find plenty of hundred-dollar bills, all new. He then counted the dollar bills individually to find $400,000 in the bag. He was stunned. He wanted to shout but was afraid to bring the Apartment Management in. The first idea that came through his was to take the black leather bag and the money far away from his hosts' eyes. Miguel put the black bag with the money in a bookbag, closed the apartment door, and walked fifteen minutes to a T-Mobil shop in a giant shopping center. He purchased the latest iPhone and had an international access line. When he exited the T-Mobil shop, Miguel called his mother in El Salvador for the first time alone. He told his mother he was planning to return home and would ship his clothes and belongings to her. His mother didn't know what to make of the news. Should she be happy or sad? What happened to her son to make a drastic decision to go back to El Salvador? Miguel walked into another store next to the T-Mobil shop to wire $1,000 through Western Union to his mother while she was still on the phone. He communicated the transfer number to his mother and instructed her to use the money for her needs, such as clothing and food.

Miguel's unwavering sense of responsibility towards his family always weighed heavily on his shoulders, but the expenses in the apartment made it hard for him to save any money. After he had relieved his mother's burden, Miguel requested a UBER to take him to a public self-storage at 4140 Cherry Avenue, Long Beach. He rented a unit of 5 feet over 10 feet for $130 a month. He signed a six-month contract that he paid in full. He bought three padlocks and a couple of boxes from the operation store on the premises. He put a padlock on the black leather bag and two padlocks on his self-storage unit and put the keys in his pocket. Miguel came back to the apartment in UBER as if nothing had happened.

He resumed his work activities with his hosts, who saw no changes in Miguel's behavior.

Miguel took a day off work a week later to take care of some business. He went to the mall to purchase a pair of black tennis shoes for himself and women's clothing for his mother and younger sister. He threw all the clothing in a shipping box and carefully laid the black tennis shoes in the middle. Miguel inserted an envelope with $20,000 inside the black tennis shoes. He waited three weeks to ensure his mother received the box in good condition before sending another one. After three weeks, his mother sent him pictures and a video of the condition of the box containing the clothing. Miguel felt a sense of relief and accomplishment knowing that his plan had worked. He would send his mother a box containing $50,000 monthly without forgetting his month's $1,000 Western Union wire transfer for personal use. Miguel managed to send all the money to his mother in a black leather bag for six months. His mother stocked the boxes in the room he occupied before he left the country for the United States.

In the last month of his stay, Miguel summoned his hosts to announce his return to El Salvador. They were shocked and dismayed to see someone throw away all the opportunities in America and return to problems. They tried to get the reasons for his decision out of his mouth but were unsuccessful. Miguel's decision touched Rosa the most because she loved him secretly and expected a serious relationship. At the end of the sixth month, Miguel took a bus to Tijuana and flew from Mexico City to San Salvador International Airport. His mother and younger sister jumped on him at the airport, hugged and kissed him. His mother was sharing a tear of rejoicing, and his younger sister was laughing joyfully. They drove all bouncing and singing in the car to their San Vicente home. Miguel was shocked to see his mother renovating the house he used to live in. With the money he sent her, she made a new roof to the house and covered the roof with solar panels, providing continuous electricity. She took Miguel to his room and presented him with all the boxes he had been sending for six months. Miguel opened the boxes one by one and handed the clothes still in plastic to his mother and sister. The ladies were jumping, hugging, and kissing one another without expecting a final surprise coming out of the black tennis shoes. When Miguel retrieved all the money in the black shoes and put it in his mother's hands, she fainted on the ground. After fifteen minutes of ventilation, she came back in total disbelief. To his mother and younger sister, Miguel revealed in detail his plan of producing coffee beans on the 10 acres of land his father left for them.

A week after his return, Miguel went to the Department of Agriculture in San Salvador's agricultural equipment division to order a Caterpillar Front-End Loader for about $40,000. He also went to the farm department to order young coffee plants for his 10 acres of land and purchased an irrigation system from Kifco Inc. for $37,000. The young coffee plants would start producing in three years, and he had enough money to sustain the family for the time being. His determination was unwavering, his commitment absolute. Within 30 days, Caterpillar delivered the Front-End Loader to Mr. Escobar's farm. Miguel used the tractor to clear bushes over the farm his father left for the family. After providing the young coffee plants, he hired people working on farms to help him plant the young coffee plants to cover the 10 acres. The Kifco company sent some professional technicians to install their irrigation system to water every little coffee plant on the farm. They used a solar system to water the farm every morning at 5:00 a.m. automatically and every evening at 6:00 p.m. continuously. After three years of persistent care, Miguel's farm became green with abundant coffee beans. The farm flourished so much that the El Salvador government sent some officials to sign a contract with Miguel, who supplied coffee beans to the government every year.

Chapter 23

Lawrence and Anke in
Sydney, Australia

The Australian Prime Minister called the White House to complain about work performed by the Cork Theory agent sent to Sydney in the investigation into the death of Tony Hewitt, an international tennis player. The White House summoned the FBI director, Max Richardson, to resolve the issue. Mr. Richardson called Lawrence Jackson for an urgent meeting in his Washington, DC, office the following day. Mr. Richardson arranged a particular plan and a limousine to bring Lawrence to his office with some other FBI counsels. But before Lawrence could make it to his boss's office, Keith Ross called from Sydney to explain the problem he encountered. Only one tree was in front of the tennis player's house at 39 Harden Cres, Georges Hall. The house had a two-car garage with a long driveway to get to the house. On the far left of the house was a small path leading to the back of the house. The tree in front of the house was well-positioned to record anyone going into the tennis player's house on foot or by car.

When Mr. Keith Ross came, the Australian Federal Police Chief of Staff, Brian Reese, received him at the Sydney International Airport and lodged him at the Four Seasons Hotel. It was one of the prestigious hotels in Australia where Mr. Reese booked the tenth floor exclusively for Mr. Keith Ross to complete the investigation promptly. Mr. Ross cut all the cork from the tree before the tennis player's domicile for two weeks. He inserted the corks in a MgSO4 solution with red vinegar, but no images were generated. He repeated the experiment several times, but no positive results were recorded. He cut some branches of the tree, thinking they would yield a better outcome, but the copy papers stayed blank after drying. Besides, the Australian Prime Minister would call Keith Ross every day to get the results of his experiment. The national opinion pressed the prime Minister to find the perpetrator of the crime and punish him with a maximum prison term. It was a horrifying crime against the beloved tennis player, who was stabbed multiple times with a knife in his living room.

The following day, Lawrence took a flight from Dulles Airport to Reagan National Airport, where FBI agents were waiting for him in a black bulletproof limousine. In Max Richardson's office, his vice director and some government cabinet members were waiting to get a good explanation of the situation. Lawrence took the time to explain the problem and the challenges facing the agent in Sydney. In addition to the ordeal, he proposed flying to Australia in three days to correct the problem. A bright smile rolled over the face of the FBI director and all the officials at the meeting because they acknowledged the effectiveness of Lawrence's contribution to the agency. Lawrence Jackson exposed to the audience the danger that his job performance entailed and requested security protection for his whole family. He asked that his wife follow him whenever he was staying in a hotel to conduct the investigation. In addition, he needed security protection over his house and two children. He expressed concern about retaliation from the hands of criminals who wouldn't like to be prosecuted for their crimes. In the presence of the government officials, Mr. Max Richardson was guaranteed to have FBI agents guard Lawrence's house and children. He made the guarantee in writing, gave a copy to Lawrence, and kept copies for the agency. Before the meeting ended, a flight to Sydney International Airport was booked for Lawrence and his wife, and a copy of the itinerary and a confirmation of his arrival in Sydney in three days were sent to the prime Minister.

In three days, Lawrence and Anke packed their luggage and boarded an Air New Zealand flight to Sydney International Airport, where the Australian Federal Chief Police, Brian Reese and Keith Ross, were expecting them. Mr. Brian Reese rushed Lawrence to the Four Seasons Hotel on the tenth floor to assess the situation and correct the problem. Mr. Keith Ross took Lawrence to every container of $MgS0_4$ solution containing pieces of cork and wood in almost every room on the tenth floor. After a quick evaluation of the situation, Lawrence reassured the Chief Police and instructed Mr. Reese to take him to the crime site the following day.

The next day, at 8:30 a.m., the Australian Federal Chief Police took Lawrence and Keith to 39 Harden Cres, Georges Hall. The house was close to the public, and a force police presence was at the entrance. Lawrence saw that the only tree at the entrance had been stripped of cork and was missing some branches. Mr. Ross admitted to cutting parts of the tree to conduct his unsuccessful experiments. Before entering the house of the crime, Lawrence realized that an intuition that enacted him activated strongly in him. The intuition was pushing him toward a flower picture on the wall. While the police detectives at the site showed photos of the crime scene, Lawrence's eyes were drawn to the flower picture. He removed the image from the wall and covered it with a plastic back. As soon as he removed the picture, an immense joy came over him and went from his head to his feet. After observing the crime scene photos, Lawrence returned to the hotel with pleasure, knowing how to resolve the situation.

Lawrence took Anke to a supermarket in Downtown Sydney to purchase some articles. They went to Coles Pyrmont Supermarket to buy a transparent plastic container for the frame he had taken from the tennis player's house. They also purchased two bottles of red vinegar and a pack of copy paper to launch the cork experiment. Lawrence and his wife rushed back to the hotel, where he was staying in his room on the tenth floor, to start his experiment. Lawrence prepared a solution of $MgSO4$ with the red vinegar in the transparent plastic container purchased at Coles Supermarket. He inserted the frame of the picture he had taken from the tennis player's wall in the solution. He left the solution and the frame in a dark closet of his hotel room for 24 hours. After securing the closet and the hotel room, Anke and Lawrence took the elevator to the hotel lobby, where a government vehicle was at their service for 24 hours. The car took them to the Queen Victoria Mall, where Anke loved shopping. For the whole evening, Anke took Lawrence to various department stores in the Queen Victoria Mall. She purchased beautiful women's clothes, shoes, hats, and gloves. Before she put an end to her shopping spree, Anke spotted a charming restaurant. They went in and enjoyed eating different kinds of steak and grilled lobsters. When they returned to the Four Seasons Hotel, Mr. Keith Ross cleaned all the mess he made in every room on the tenth floor and caught his flight back to the US.

The following day, around noon, Lawrence went into the closet to retrieve the plastic container containing the MgS04 solution covering the picture frame taken from Mr. Tony Hewitt's house. He put the container on a table next to the TV in the room, where he had a stack of copy papers for the experiment. Lawrence gently dropped copy papers on the solution's surface to collect the image deposited in the solution. Lawrence gently collected 20 photos and dried them in the closet for two hours. He couldn't recognize anyone in the pictures but could see the crime scene unfolding clearly. He could explain to his wife, Anke, what took place in Mr. Tony Hewitt's house leading to his death. Anke asked him why he decided to take the flower picture frame among all the pictures on the wall in the tennis player's room. Lawrence couldn't answer his wife's question and paused momentarily. In the moment of pause, Lawrence realized he had an intuition inside of him that would lead him to cut a specific area of a tree cork. Each time he cut the right portion of a tree cork for his experiment; a feeling of joy covered him. Every time he sectioned the wrong portion of a tree cork for his experiment, bitterness overcame his body. The same intuition drew him to the flower picture frame on the tennis player's house wall. After he took the flower picture frame, a joyful feeling came to him as he wrapped the frame in a plastic bag.

Lawrence called in Mr. Brian Reese, Australian Federal Chief Police, who rushed to the hotel with two other Australian Police Detectives. Lawrence sat them on a table in the hotel room to review the pictures one after one to reconstruct the crime scene. The images revealed two people drove to the tennis player's house and parked in the driveway. The first person, a lady of about 26 years, rang the doorbell, and Mr. Hewitt opened the door after a moment of hesitation. The two persons knew each other and started arguing about something. The second person in the car, a male of about 35 years, came to the scene with a long kitchen knife in his pocket. All of a sudden, the 35-year-old man reached for the knife in his pocket and stabbed the tennis player in the stomach twice. Mr. Tony Hewitt crumbled on the floor with two hands on his stomach. The man proceeded to stab his victim several times in the back and on the head. Mr. Hewitt lay inert in a pool of his blood when the two perpetrators walked out of the house as if nothing had happened. The tennis player was in the pool of blood until the following day when his new girlfriend came in to call the police. Mr. Brian Reese and his colleagues were very impressed by the art of crime scene reconstruction Lawrence possessed.

Mr. Reese took the 20 pictures back to his office at the Police Headquarters in Sydney, Australia, for further investigation. He then assembled a team of prosecutors, investigators, and magistrates to tackle the case diligently. He searched the Police mugshot database for facial identification, which turned out to be negative. No one seemed to recognize the young lady and the man in the photos Lawrence got from his cork experiment. The Police Chief didn't want to unveil the investigation by showing the two suspects to the public.

The idea came to his mind to find the victim's father, who lived in northern Australia, for help. Mr. Brian Reese sent the victim's father two police officers with the photo of the two suspects. The two officers found him in his house in Darwin, Australia. They presented him with the two suspects in the death of his son, Tony Hewitt. He recognized the woman in the photo as the ex-girlfriend of his deceased son. Her name was Yvonne Rocher, and she was very controlling in the relationship and couldn't digest the fact Mr. Tony Hewitt dumped her for another woman. Returning from Darwin, the two officers searched Yvonne Rocher's driving record to find all her contacts. They secured an arrest warrant from a judge and went to Yvonne Rocher's house early in the morning. She had just woke up to get ready to go to work when the two police officers knocked at her single apartment door. After being presented with the arrest warrant, she was handcuffed and taken to police custody. Yvonne Rocher refused to talk at the interrogation table and requested the presence of an attorney. After two days of pressure in police custody, she finally wrote on a piece of paper the complete name of her associate in crime. The stabbing man's name was Kerry London. He got picked up and jailed at the police station, waiting for a trial. The Prime Minister was briefed on every investigation step and refused any possible bail for the violent criminals. He suggested that the two suspects be judged in a Commonwealth Court for a maximum penalty. The government assigned an attorney for the two defenders, who finally pleaded guilty to the crime because of the overwhelming evidence against them. A Commonwealth Judge sentenced Kerry London to 25 years in prison and Yvonne Rocher to 20 years. The Australian Prime Minister was very delighted with the outcome of the case. He paid the

White House all the expenses of the two Cork Agents and a month's salary.

Meanwhile, Anke received a flyer in Code's Supermarket for a performance at the Sydney Opera House, a magnificent building located on the foreshore of Sydney Harbor. She was nagging her husband to take her to the performance of "Sunset Boulevard." It was a sung-through musical with music by Andrew Lloyd Webber and lyrics and libretto by Don Black. Anke loved the place, which for her was an architectural marvel where she dinned with Lawrence the last day before they returned to Virginia. Anke took many unforgettable pictures of Sydney Harbor and purchased many articles for souvenir. The Sydney Harbor was very magnificent at night with beautiful lights reflecting on the surface of the water all night long.

Chapter 24

Lawrence became the only agent in the Cork Department.

B efore Lawrence returned to the U.S., many complaints were filed against his theory—many F.B.I. Agents who attended Lawrence's class on the Cork Theory reported the theory's inefficiency to the agency director—many agents who came to the training sessions held on the seventh floor of the F.B.I. Forensic Lab needed help to practice what they had learned. Every state in the union sent two F.B.I. agents to Lawrence Jackson's Cork Theory training to understand how the theory worked. After the training, all the agents returned to their respective states to practice the theory, but unfortunately, they all failed. Some agents had burning cases to crack but could not retrieve images from the MgSO4 solutions. Others returned to their states to try the theory and realized something was missing from the training. They cut three branches, leaves, roots, and corks, but none couldn't do the work. Very tired and disturbed, the agent reported that Mr. Max Richardson didn't understand what was happening.

On the first day of Lawrence's return to work after his victorious work in Australia, Mr. Max Richardson paid him an earnest visit—the F.B.I. The Director was very anxious, so he exposed the complaints sent to him in Lawrence Jackson's absence. To alleviate the Director's anxiety, Lawrence expended on the problems of why the other agents couldn't succeed in extracting images. He explained the feeling that always guided him in choosing the cork portion to cut. He believed that was the missing element in the life of the F.B.I. agents who attempted to practice the Cork Theory. Lawrence explained that intuition led him to solve the Australian tennis player's case. In Sydney, he realized he didn't need a tree before I could find the pictures of the crime scenes. He could collect the images from any object his intuition led him to. Lawrence could reconstruct any crime scene if his intuition led him to an object that recorded the scene. Mr. Max Richardson was very impressed by the ability that Lawrence engorged and his confidence in his ability to solve any crime. The F.B.I. director spoke to Lawrence Jackson about a burning case in Los Angeles that needed an urgent resolution.

- "There is an urgent case in Los Angeles," Mr. Richardson said.
- "What kind of case is it? Lawrence asked.
- "The Major of Los Angeles calls me to request our assistance," Mr. Richardson continued.
- "What happened in Los Angeles? Lawrence inquired.
- "The secretary of the Mayor's office was stabbed to death in her bedroom." Mr. Richardson added.
- "When did that happen?" Lawrence asked.
- "The body was found this morning," Mr. Richardson continued, looking deep into Lawrence's eyes.
- "If the crime area is well preserved, I'll solve it," affirmed Lawrence.

Mr. Max Richardson was thrilled about Lawrence's availability to crack the case in Los Angeles. He called the Los Angeles Mayor to reassure him that he was sending him one of his best agents to solve the issue. He insisted the house of the crime be well taped and every little item preserved. Mr. Richardson prepared himself for the trip for Lawrence and his wife to Los Angeles. He booked the flight, the hotel, the security, and the expenses for Lawrence and his wife.

The next day, early in the morning, Lawrence and Anke flew to L.A.X. International Airport. Lawrence ensured he had the necessary equipment to operate the Cork Theory. Their flight landed around 3:00 p.m. California Time. The Los Angeles Police Chief welcomed them in the airport hall and presented them to the two L.A.P.D. officers who would ensure their security in L.A. He had at their disposal a non-marked police vehicle and two L.A.P.D. officers. The two officers were supposed to follow Lawrence and Anke wherever they went. One officer, officer Bolton, would drive them, and the second one, officer Cooper, would sit beside them. From the airport, the Los Angeles Police Chief took them to the Hilton Hotel on Wilshire Boulevard. The Police Chief booked the third floor of the Hilton hotel to Lawrence to avoid interference and disturbance. The Police Chief took Lawrence to South Central, where the crime occurred. The house was sealed completely, and no one could go in except the police forces around the house. The Police Chief led Lawrence Jackson through the presence of the police forces and took him into the room where the dead body was found. As Lawrence's foot entered the crime scene, he got drawn onto a white clock on the wall. Although many other photos of the victim were on the wall, the intuition inside Lawrence was so strong toward the white clock that he took it and covered it with plastic. The Police Chief narrated the circumstances of the death of the Major's secretary, Mrs. Vasquez.

Mrs. Vasquez lived with her older daughter, Andrea, a registered nurse at a large hospital in Los Angeles. Andrea had three sons who were old and had moved out to get their apartments. From time to time, Andrea's three sons visited their mother and grandmother. Andrea preferred working day shifts at the hospital because she didn't like leaving her mother, who was 65 years old, at home alone. The job duties obliged Andrea to work a graveyard shift once every two weeks. Andrea took on a twelve-hour overnight shift and came home early in the morning to see her mother dead in her bedroom. She was stabbed several times in the stomach and the back. Andrea called the police when she saw her mother lying on the floor in a pool of blood. She also called the Los Angeles Mayor's office to report the loss. The mayor couldn't digest the loss of Mrs. Vasquez, the backbone of the local government of the City of Los Angeles. Who would want the death of such a loving and caring person the mayor admired so much for her dedication and experience? Mrs. Vasquez worked as the Los Angeles Mayor's secretary all her life. She knew her job very well and did it with passion and devotion. When the police came to preserve the crime scene, they removed Andrea and put her in a Motel 6 until investigation completed.

When Lawrence returned to his hotel room, where Anke was waiting impatiently, he launched his experiment to crack Mrs. Vasquez's case. He unpacked his toolbox and retrieved a plastic container in which he created a solution of $MgSO_4$. He added two bottles of red vinegar to the solution and emerged the white clock he took from Mrs. Vasquez's bedroom. Lawrence carefully deposited the container with all the elements in a dark closet of his hotel room. He locked the closet firmly and took Anke to the hotel restaurant on the first floor. The couple enjoyed their meal and bought gifts for one another to candle the love that embraced them. When it was getting dark, Lawrence and Anke went back to their hotel room on the third floor. Soon after they returned to their hotel room, they heard a knock on the door. The Los Angeles mayor and his wife visited them to get to know Lawrence and his wife very well. The Mayor had heard much about Lawrence and his Cork Theory, and international recognition granted him worldwide. The two couples had a very amicable evening until late at night. The Mayor expressed joy for the presence of Lawrence in L.A. because the crime rate in the city was alarming. Gang activities in Los Angeles overpowered the police forces and help from the Federal government was deeply appreciated. Delighted of their presence, the Mayor promised to take Lawrence and his wife to various fun places in Los Angeles and surrounding areas. He vowed to take them to the Universal Studio Hollywood and the Disney World in Orange County. The Mayor and his wife left the Jacksons delighted with the visit and expected to hang out with them soon.

The next day, at noon, Lawrence retrieved his experiment from the closet and used copy paper to collect the images yielded on the solution's surface. The pictures were clear and neatly described the event that led to the death of the Mayor's secretary. He collected 12 photos relevant to the murder of Mrs. Vasquez. Lawrence called the Los Angeles Police Chief, who didn't hesitate to rush to the hotel room.

He couldn't believe his eyes. The pictures are related to the confrontation between the victim and her murderer. The murderer was a young man of about 24 years old, very slim, and left-handed. The Police Chief believed that the suspect might know the victim and that the victim's daughter, Andrea, might recognize him. The Police Chief didn't want to waste a minute. He jumped into his vehicle with his driver ready on the stirring wheel. Lawrence hopped in his unmarked police car with Officer Bolton on the wheel and Officer Cooper beside him. The LAPD officers were heavily armed and followed the Police Chief to Motel 6, where Ms. Andrea was living temporarily. She was sitting on the bed when the Police Chief and Lawrence entered the motel room. They presented her with one photo of the perpetrator to see if she could identify the person.

Andrea screamed when she recognized her younger son, Lorenzo. After controlling her emotions, she gave Lorenzo's address in Inglewood, where he shared an apartment with his friend. Lorenzo and his roommate were active members of the Black Stone Gang, which terrorized the city of Los Angeles and was involved in many crimes across the city. While he was consoling the victim's daughter, the Chief of Police sent officers Bolton and Cooper cuffed Lorenzo to the police headquarters on First Street. In the trunk of Lorenzo's car, the officers found a bloody T-shirt they took for a DNA test. Before the suspect arrived at the police Headquarters, Lawrence and the Chief of Police set up the interrogation room. The interrogation room was 8' x 10' on the second floor of the police headquarters. The walls and ceiling were well insulated to dampen outside noises and considerably lightened. The ceiling was perfectly crafted, with surveillance cameras hidden among the light bulls. The room had two chairs and a table in the middle. Lorenzo was sitting on a chair with his two hands crossed on the table in the middle of the interrogation room. Lawrence entered the interrogation room with the twelve crime scene photos and presented himself to the suspect. The Chief of Police was watching and listening to the conversation between the suspect and Lawrence.

- "We know what has happened between you and your grandmother," stated Lawrence.
- "I have nothing to do with her death," affirmed Lorenzo.
- "We want to know your side of the story," added Lawrence, who started to display the first four pictures of the crime scene before the suspect.
- "I was there for a short period, and I left," Lorenzo tried to defend himself.

"You two were arguing, and you went to the kitchen to get a long knife," Lawrence displayed the following four pictures before Lorenzo.

- "I didn't mean to. I wanted some money," Lorenzo's voice cracked, his throat tightened, and he couldn't watch the pictures before him. Tears started dripping uncontrollably from his eyes, and he held his head with two hands, hitting the table before him. Lawrence reached out to keep Lorenzo's head and removed the pictures from the table. When he came down, Lawrence gave him a sheet of paper to make a short statement of what had happened. He wrote he was doing drugs with his friends, but they didn't have enough for everybody. He promised his friends he would get some money and come back. When he asked his grandmother for some money, she refused to give it to him. He became distraught and didn't know when he grabbed a knife from the kitchen. At the end of Lorenzo's statement, an LAPD officer came in to handcuff the suspect, who asked a favor to call his friends and family members. Lorenzo called the Chief of the Black Stone Gang, Oscar.

Lawrence went to the Chief of Police, who was passionately following the interrogation, and handed him the suspect's conviction statement. He hugged Lawrence tightly for a moment to thank him for his involvement in the case. He took Lawrence to his office to show him all the unsolved cases against the Black Stone Gang. The LAPD couldn't solve the cases for fear of retaliation from the gang members. In his office, in the presence of Lawrence, the Chief of Police called the Mayor of Los Angeles to inform him of the breakthrough. He told him of the bloody shirt found in the suspect's car that had been processed in the laboratory for a DNA test. After the test would confirm the blood belonged to Mrs. Vasquez, the case would be turned to the court system. The Chief Police called in Officer Bolton and Cooper to drive Lawrence Jackson back to the Hilton hotel in the Wilshire District. Officer Bolton was driving the vehicle, and Officer Cooper, sitting next to Lawrence, showed him different important buildings in Los Angeles. After about fifteen minutes of driving, Lawrence realized a Black Cadillac Deville was following them. Lawrence was paying close attention to the movement of the black Cadillac with two passengers and a driver. All three occupants of the Cadillac were young adult males of about twenty-three years of age. All of a sudden, the Black Cadillac speeded up to the driver's side of the unmarked police car, and the two passengers opened fire in the direction of where Lawrence was sitting. Because he was observing them, Lawrence quickly bent down to the back seat, and the bullets hit Officer Cooper. He fell over Lawrence, who lay flat on the back seat.

Officer Bolton called for backup while bullets were raining through the back windows of the unmarked police car. The bullets were aimed at Lawrence, but Officer Cooper took all the bullets and died on the spot. Office Bolton managed to control the vehicle and chased down the Black Cadillac Deville, which was trying to escape. The LAPD helicopter overflew the city and spotted the Black Cadillac on South Rampart Boulevard. Officer Bolton kept following the Black Cadillac, calling for backup and giving up the Cadillac's direction. Seven police swat vehicles were released, and five police cars launched the chase against the three criminals. They were chased from the air and the road throughout the city's major highway for two hours. The chase ended when the Cadillac hit an electric pole, and the three criminals surrendered. They were arrested, and multiple weapons and ammunition were uncovered in the Black Cadillac Deville. The three suspects were charged with murder and tentative of murder. They all belonged to the Black Stone Gang of Los Angeles and operated out of an abandoned warehouse in South Central.

During the high-speed chase, Officer Bolton pulled the unmarked police car to the side to assess the damage. He opened the back door to see Officer Cooper lying on Lawrence Jackson, who was covered entirely with the Officer's blood.

Officer Bolton called for an ambulance and reported on the radio the death of Officer Cooper. Other LAPD Officers came out to Bolton's side to attest to the death of their colleague Cooper. The ambulance came in and pronounced Officer Cooper dead in the line of duty. Lawrence went out of the vehicle untouched but socked wet with blood. He was trembling and couldn't believe he had escaped the ordeal alive. The unmarked police car was severely damaged. All the back windows were gone due to the flying bullets. Another police Officer had to take Lawrence back to the hotel, where his wife Anke watched the live high-speed chase on KTLA Live News. Lawrence didn't have words to narrate to his wife how close he was to death and the loss of the kind and caring Officer Cooper. The event haunted him so much that he decided to do something to solve the Gang violence in Los Angeles.

The next day, first thing in the morning, Lawrence went to the Chief of Police to grant him access to the police equipment. He went to the new LAPD shooting range facility in the North of Los Angeles for two days to sharpen his shooting abilities. On the evening of the second day of his firearm proficiency training, Lawrence took a squat team to visit the Black Stone Gang in a meeting in their abandoned warehouse. The squat team surrendered the old warehouse to apprehend any escapees. About ten of them met with the Chief Gang Oscar in front, who was informing the group about Lorenzo's arrest and elaborating on a plan to kidnap or hold hostage Lawrence's wife. When Oscar saw Lawrence in the warehouse, he shot at him, but Lawrence was quicker to get him in the leg. Realizing the presence of the LAPD, the rest of the Gang members fled the location to be apprehended outside by the squat team. All of them were taken into police custody. Then, the squat team came inside the abandoned warehouse to search the whole location for anything that could convince the gang members in a court of law. They found handguns and ammunition used in different crimes committed across the city. They also found the names and addresses of businesses the Gang members robbed in the past. The list of the names of the Gang members was also found hidden under a blanket in a dirty warehouse room. Lawrence brought all the findings to the Los Angeles Chief of Police and was determined to bring justice to every Gang member. The Black Stone Gang had a total of seventy-two members. Lawrence was determined to bring them to justice one after one. When the Gang members heard that their Chief Oscar was in police custody and that the LAPD was after them, they all fled town. Every Gang member's house Lawrence went to, people said they packed their belongings and left town overnight. The "Los Angeles Times" devised a big front-page title, "The Dissolving Black Stone Gang," where Lawrence Jackson's helping hand lifted the LAPD to glory.

Chapter 25

Lawrence, a family man.

Returning to Virginia, Lawrence saw his picture on the Richmond Times front page as the news organization related the Los Angeles Times news about the Black Stone Gang. Some Los Angeles Times news anchors followed some gang members to their new locations. Some moved to Denver, Colorado, and some to Reno, Nevada. The Black Stone Gang activities were nonexistent in the great Los Angeles, and the inhabitants regained the peace of mind they had lost for many years.

Lawrence realized his popularity would jeopardize his life and decided to tighten the security around him and his family. He donated his Silver Nissan Morano to a charity for a better vehicle for the challenges ahead. He called the Chevrolet Dealer Ship to recommend a brand-new Chevy Tahoe with bulletproof windows. The Tahoe would cost $120,000 from a Manassas Chevy Dealer. As money wasn't the issue, Lawrence bought two Chevy Tahoe, one for himself and one for Anke. He took Anke in his new Chevy Tahoe to visit his rental property in Arlington and Alexandria. The two rental properties were doing well, yielding around $100,000 monthly. On their way back from Alexandria, Lawrence got a phone call from his ex-wife, and he put her on speakerphone so Anke could listen to the conversation.

"Hello, who is this?" Lawrence answered the call.

"It's me, Bernice," the female voice on the other end replied.

"What's up, Bernice?" Lawrence was looking into Anke's face with widened eyes.

"Your children have been out of school for two weeks now. They bother me every day to come to you," Bernice explained.

"Oh, I forget all about my promise to them. Why they didn't call me?" Lawrence asked.

"Their grandparents confiscated their phones so they could study."

"Alright, I'm going to purchase their plane ticket tomorrow and make a flight reservation for next week," Lawrence affirmed.

"Hold it right there!" Bernice interrupted.

"I'm not going to let my kids move to a place I don't know," Bernice interjected with a strong pitch in her voice.

"What do you mean, Bernice?" Lawrence continued.

"You need to buy three plane tickets and one for me, or they won't be coming," Bernice added to make her point.

"But, how long are you going to stay?" Lawrence wanted to make sure.

"I need to bring them myself, and I need just a week's stay," Bernice answered.

"Okay, I'll send you the confirmation and artillery tomorrow," while looking into Anke's face for a sign of objection.

Anke wasn't too happy about the call. She didn't like the idea that Bernice would live with them for a week, so she proposed renting a hotel room for her. Anke didn't want to see her husband's ex-wife residing under the same roof as her. A female instinct warned her of danger, but she didn't know how to explain it to her husband. Lawrence reassured her several times that there was no feeling of attachment between him and Bernice. The latter had a different view of the link between the two. Since the day Josh and Grace narrated with emotion all the fun, they had the last time they visited Lawrence, she changed her heart. The children related vividly to their good times at the Virginia Zoo, the Virginia Aquarium, and Virginia Beach. At the ultimate climax of their enjoyment was the Sunday afternoon fun activities with pastor Carlos Montpelier's children. Bernice changed her heart when she realized that Lawrence was living large with his new wife, Anke. She firmly believed that enjoyment should be hers and was willing to try any canny devices to lure Lawrence into her arms.

The following day of Bernice's call, Lawrence purchased three plane tickets and forwarded the itinerary and flight information to Bernice. Bernice was excited about the trip, hoping her secret plan to seduce Lawrence would work. She bought brand new suitcases for the two children and put them in their best clothes. Bernice summoned her parents to demand the return of the confiscated phones. She wasn't on good terms with Liz and Andrew since she learned how large Lawrence and Anke lived. She blamed her parents for pushing her to divorce Lawrence in prison and marry a poor preacher. Although the poor preacher objected to the trip, Bernice didn't pay him any mind. On the day of the departure, Bernice dropped the child she had with Mr. Leonardo James, the poor preacher, with her parents. It was a Saturday afternoon, and Lawrence didn't go to work. He went to the airport to pick up his two children and their mother. Lawrence went to the airport alone while Anke stayed behind to cook her delicious meals for the guests. Lawrence welcomed them to the Dulles International Airport Hall. The kids were jumping with gleam to see their father again.

After they retrieved their respective suitcases, he took them to his Chevy Tahoe parked in the vast airport parking lot. Bernice was stunned to see Lawrence's ride. She said to herself:" Definitively, this is wealthy." The outside of the SUV was black, but the inside was all genuine leather. The interior was spacious, with a lovely golden carpet engraved with the word "Tahoe." It had 72 cubic feet of cargo space when the third row was down to accommodate all the suitcases. Bernice had three suitcases as if she didn't intend to return to Georgia. The two front seats had a small TV screen to entertain the occupants in the back seats for a long-distance trip. When Bernice tried to beg Lawrence to take her back, Josh and Grace were cruising comfortably in the back seats, separately watching their favorite cartoon with headphones on. She complained that her divorce was the work of her mother, Liz, and she didn't want to go that route, but her parents pushed her to. Lawrence tried to reason with Bernice in her request but wouldn't comply. She was so determined in her reconciliation with Lawrence that she wouldn't take no for an answer. So, Lawrence asked her:

"Okay, what do you want me to do with Anke when you come in?"

"Kick that bitch out," Bernice firmly replied.

"That won't happen today or tomorrow," Lawrence affirmed in an authoritarian voice.

Then, there was complete silence in the vehicle, with only the gentile sound of the air conditioning through the Chevy Tahoe. When they drove to Lawrence's residence in Dumfries, Bernice saw another brand-new Chevy Tahoe parked inside the driveway. She was about to faint and drop to the ground when she heard the other Tahoe belonged to Anke. Bernice wanted to slap herself on the cheek for missing out on the opportunities. Anke welcomed them and took Bernice's suitcases to the guest room while the kids went upstairs to their rooms. Anke dressed at a table for them in the living room, and she displayed all her best cooking: pasta lasagna, ravioli, pizza, mac, and cheese, along with many soft drinks. They all ate satisfactorily and watched TV until late that night before everyone slept.

The same day Bernice arrived; Lawrence received a summons to appear in court in Los Angeles. Lorenzo and Oscar's lawyers formed a coalition to discredit the Cork Theory in court. The two lawyers believed that Lawrence's works had no scientific foundation and that it shouldn't be acceptable for a person to be convinced in a court of law. The same evening, Lawrence called the Los Angeles mayor to share the case with him. The Mayor promised to find him an excellent attorney to represent him in court. He also called the Los Angeles Chief of Police to brief him on the court order. He also ensured Lawrence that he would find him a good lawyer with a good track record. The Chief of Police informed Lawrence of the upcoming funeral and burial of Officer Cooper, who laid down his life for him. Lawrence's mind went back to the moment his unmarked police car came under fire from Los Angeles gang members. A dreadful feeling of death went through him, and he promised the Chief of Police to be at the funeral. The following Monday, Lawrence faxed the court documents to his boss, Mr. Max Richardson, and requested time off to go to Los Angeles.

Before Bernice's visit ended, Anke hired a lovely lady, Ms. Nicole, from her church as a nanny for the children. She would work for ten hours a day, from Monday through Friday, from six in the morning to six in the afternoon. Nicole accepted the job with a decent salary and was ready to start when Bernice vacated the guest room. Nicole would get $2000 every two weeks plus extra cash if she had to stay over. Ms. Nicole's responsibility was to take care of the children's basic needs. She would wake them up in the morning and prepare them to go to school on time. She would wash their clothes and arrange their beds as needed. Ms. Nicole would wash the dishes, vacuum the carpet, remove the trash, and make the house neat. Bernice would like to take Nicole's job and earn $4000 a month, but she knew Lawrence would never allow that to happen. Bernice attempted to seduce Lawrence three times and was successful. Three times, she went into the master room upstairs while Anke was cooking in the kitchen to try to rob Lawrence.

Lawrence didn't make any noises during the three attempts but quietly walked away from Bernice to hug his wife in the kitchen. The day Bernice left the residence, Lawrence called an Uber to take her to the Dulles International Airport to catch her flight back to Georgia. His alibi was that he was preparing to fly to California for a critical meeting with police officials in Los Angeles.

The following Tuesday, the Tuesday of Bernice's departure, Lawrence and Anke dressed like bright, shining stars on a hill. They flew a rented private jet to LAX International Airport, where a rental limousine awaited them. Lawrence wore a designer three-piece suit in black with a cozy texture, a plain white shirt, and a slim black tie. To maintain his respectful appearance, Lawrence wore sunglasses. On the other hand, Anke was dazzling in a down-to-earth, stylish Louis Vuiton black outfit she bought in Sydney, Australia. The limousine dropped them off at the 3600 Crenshaw Boulevard, Los Angeles funeral service venue. The big Crenshaw Boulevard wasn't accessible to traffic, and only funeral attendees could pass through. The West Angeles Cathedrale was full of people from all over the Great Los Angeles to pay respect to a fallen LAPD Office Cooper. The service for Office Cooper began before Lawrence and Anke entered the Cathedrale. An usher led them to the front seats reserved for the dignities and state officials. LAPD Officers occupied the middle column seats of the church in uniform. Many of them were still mourning and weeping for their fallen colleague. Officer Cooper's casket lay on a table below the church platform, and the USA flag covered it all around. The Los Angeles Mayor, the Chief of Police, some movie stars, and basketball players of the Lakers were present at the funeral. The sounds of the gun salute sent a chill throughout the Cathedrale, and crying and weeping intensified in the audience. Some close colleagues of Officer Cooper went up to the pulpit to give an account of Officer Cooper's love for his job and the city. Indeed, he had impacted many LAPD Officers around, and he trained and supported many of them who were speechless before the tragedy that took his life.

At the end of the service, the West Angeles Cathedrale Bishop gave an overview of the fallen police Officer's performance during his twelve years of service. He left behind a wife and two daughters who were still in college. The Bishop closed his sermon with instructions on how to exit the Cathedrale and a list of the categories of people who would leave first. Six of the LAPD Officers took the casket on their shoulders into a black hearse waiting at the entrance of the Cathedrale to take the dead to the Los Angeles National Cemetery on Sepulveda Boulevard. After the hearse followed the vehicles of state officials, the police forces, the movie stars, the basketball players, and the rest of the audience. Lawrence and Anke rode with the Chief of Police, who was very enthusiastic about seeing them again.

Many people from around Los Angeles and beyond lined up along the funeral procession route to Sepulveda Boulevard to pay their final respects to Officer Cooper. Some on the roadside threw balloons at the passing funeral vehicle, while others threw flowers. In the cemetery, there were more gun salutes before Officer Cooper's dead body lay to rest. After the burial, the Los Angeles Chief of Police took Lawrence and Anke to the lawyer working on the lawsuit. Attorney Joseph Webster reviewed Lawrence and Lorenzo's interrogation record in his office on the corner of Oliver Street and California Avenue before the three got in. The Chief of Police surrounded all the documents and records of Lawrence's involvement in the fight against gang activities in Los Angeles. Attorney Webster studied the case against his client very well and reassured the Chief of Police and Lawrence that he would win the case in court. Lawrence called the limousine driver from the attorney's office, who came and took him and Anke back to LAX. It was late, around 7:00 p.m., when they got dropped off at the Los Angeles International Airport. Lawrence proposed to his wife to spend the night in a hotel around the airport and fly back to Virginia the next day. Although very hangry, Anke categorically refused her husband's subjection because she was scared of possible gang violence against Lawrence. So, Anke and Lawrence flew the rental private jet back to Virginia and made it home to Dumfries around 2:00 a.m. when everyone was asleep.

The case against Lawrence took about three weeks, and the judge rejected the plaintive' arguments. The plaintive' arguments weren't sufficient to convince the judge of any wrongdoing in the Cork Theory. The coalition of lawyers insisted that the theory was based on intuition and had no scientific backup, so it wasn't valid to convince a criminal. The judge didn't buy their arguments but rather exalted the number of convictions the theory generated. In closing, the judge gave Lawrence, through his attorney, full accreditation for his works.

Lawrence continued to work with the FBI to help local police forces put criminals behind bars in all fifty states of the United States of America.

Same author Philip C Sossou

Philip C. Sossou was very fascinated by literature at an early age.

He holds a master's degree in African literature from the University of Lomé. In grade school, he led some interesting research in African means of transmitting cultural values from one generation to another. In his early academic life, Philip was influenced by famous African authors like Chinua Achebe, Ngugi wa Thiongo, and Ayi Kwei Armah. Later in life, he embraced well-known American writers, namely, Helen Keller, Paul Anderson, and Henry James. From them he learned the art of creating images with words. To inspire his students to become interested in literature, he wrote a dynamic critics of Daisy Miller. As a schoolteacher, Philip encourages many of his students to develop the skill of writing essays and dissertations.

Printed in the United States
by Baker & Taylor Publisher Services